Conveniently W~~e~~...

~~Thr~~ee royal kingdoms un~~ited by~~ ~~m~~arriage—or love?

When the kingdoms of the Three Isles—Aidara, ~~Ma~~ttan and Kirtida—are threatened, for their young royal leaders duty becomes paramount. But in putting their countries first, they discover that their strategic marriages in name only run the risk of opening their guarded hearts to love...for real!

Find out more in...

United by Their Royal Baby

Childhood sweethearts Queen Leyna of Aidara and King Xavier of Mattan bear the emotional scars of ruling alone. But they now have nine months to find their way back to each other again...

Available now!

Falling for His Convenient Queen

King Zacchaeus of Kirtida and Princess Nalini of Mattan must unite their families in a marriage of convenience to secure their two kingdoms. But Nalini wants more than the cold marriage Zacchaeus has to offer. And it's up to her to rescue his heart.

Available February 2018!

Dear Reader,

Have you ever heard an author say they write what they'd like to read? Well, that's exactly what happened with the Conveniently Wed, Royally Bound duet. I created the fictional islands of Aida Mattan and Kirtida that have a shared African heritage, as I'd never read any royal romances se there. And I created diverse heroines and heroes in *United by Their Royal Baby* and *Falling for His Convenient Queen* because I'd never read royal romances where the characters looked like people in my community. Needless to say, this duet was such a pleasure to write!

United by Their Royal Baby is also special because of its characters. Leyna is one of my favorite heroines. As queen of Aidara, she's just as powerful as her hero, King Xavier of Mattan. But she's also human, torn between love and duty, as my romantic mind often imagines happens in real life. Fortunately, Xavier is perfectly matched for her. He is an alpha hero and is supportive and kind—exactly the man Leyna needs! He understands her duty, admires her strength and shows her that to be happy, they'll have to find a balance between love and duty.

Of course, their journey to happily-ever-after isn't easy. Especially with Xavier still nursing the broken heart his best friend once gave him...

You can find me on Twitter (@ThereseBeharrie), Facebook (Therese Beharrie, Author) or on my website (theresebeharrie.com).

I hope you enjoy the first of this royal duet!

Love,

Therese

United by Their Royal Baby

—

Therese Beharrie

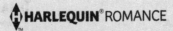
HARLEQUIN®ROMANCE

Recycling programs
for this product may
not exist in your area.

ISBN-13: 978-1-335-13498-1

United by Their Royal Baby

First North American publication 2018

Copyright © 2018 by Therese Beharrie

Printed in U.S.A.

www.Harlequin.com

Therese Beharrie has always been thrilled by romance. Her love of reading established this, and now she gets to write happily-ever-afters for a living and about all things romance in her blog at theresebeharrie.com. She married a man who constantly exceeds her romantic expectations and is an infinite source of inspiration for her romantic heroes. She lives in Cape Town, South Africa, and is still amazed that her dream of being a romance author is a reality.

Books by Therese Beharrie

Harlequin Romance

The Tycoon's Reluctant Cinderella
A Marriage Worth Saving
The Millionaire's Redemption

Visit the Author Profile page at Harlequin.com.

For Grant, the light who helps me face my fears.
Thank you for always treating me like a queen.

And Luke and Leah,
I hope when you grow up, reading books where
characters look like you is the norm. For now, this
is for you.

I love you.

Praise for
Therese Beharrie

"I really enjoyed this book. It had a gutsy,
sympathetic heroine, a moody hero, and the South
African setting was vividly drawn. A great debut
novel. I'll definitely be reading this author again."

—*Goodreads* on *The Tycoon's Reluctant Cinderella*

PROLOGUE

PRINCESS LEYNA OF AIDARA thought she'd never been more content than right at that moment. She had the sun shining on her, the ocean in front of her and the sandy beach around her.

And, of course, she had the future King of Mattan lying next to her.

'We should do this more often,' she said, and dug her back a little deeper into the sand.

'We do this at least once a week, Leyna.'

She could hear the amusement in Xavier's tone and her lips curved.

'We *visit* the beach at least once a week. Doing this—' she lifted a hand into the air and gestured to the towels that lay side by side '—is a rarity that we should definitely make more time for.'

'You're only saying that because you want to escape your royal duties,' Xavier teased.

'And you don't?' she shot back, turning her head to offer him a grin.

And ignoring the inner voice that sounded dangerously like her grandmother telling her that Xavier was an excuse to do just that.

'I'm the future King of Mattan, Princess,' he said, sarcasm dripping from his voice. 'I'm aware of my duties. Even though there are things expected of me that I can't possibly *begin* to imagine.'

Hearing the fatigue, the annoyance just beneath his words, she turned her body to face him, resting her head on her hand. 'Are your mother and grandmother at it again?'

He mirrored her position. Before she could stop herself, her eyes took in his muscular body, the dark brown hair that was a mess from their swim earlier and the kindness that was clear in every feature of his face. Her heart began to race. And then she told herself to stop it, and notice how that kindness was now eclipsed by sadness—tinged with the slightest bit of anger—that she knew came from his hopelessness about his family.

'When are they *not* at it?' He shook his head. 'Every time I think I do something right, they counter with something I should have done instead.' He paused. 'Maybe I'm just not doing anything right.'

'Oh, that's rubbish and you know it.' She sat up now, curling her legs under her. 'I've never seen someone put more effort into their crown than you have.'

'Besides you, you mean,' he said with a smile.

'Of course.' She smiled back, though the voice in her head had returned, this time telling her she would put in even more if she didn't have Xavier in her life. 'But what I meant was that that dedication already means you're doing something right, Xavier. Trust it.'

She reached over to squeeze the back of his hand, but he turned his over so quickly she didn't know it until his fingers threaded through hers. Her heart jumped, and she opened her mouth to cut off what she knew was coming.

'No,' he said before she could. 'You're not going to put me off this time, Leyna.'

'What…what do you mean?'

'I'd like you to marry me.'

Her chest tightened. 'I don't think that—'

'Both our families want this, Leyna,' he interrupted.

'They want Aidara and Mattan bonded, yes. This—you and I?' She shook her head. 'They aren't *quite* as invested in that.' When he didn't answer her, she frowned. 'You know this. You know what they think about our friendship.'

'But I know what *we* think about our friendship, too. Don't you think that's more important?'

She didn't know what to say. But she *did* know that she was glad they were on Aidara's private beach, where there would be no prying eyes witnessing their conversation.

'Leyna.' He sat up now. 'There is no choice for me. I *have* to marry you or my heart won't ever forgive me.' The seriousness in his eyes upped her heart rate even more. 'I know you feel the same way, too.'

'Why are you doing this?'

'Because it's time,' he said simply. He stood, and held out a hand to help her do the same. She took it, but when she was on her feet she snatched her hand back.

'It's time to ruin something that means more to me than anything else?'

'No. It's time to finally make this—*us*—into what we were always supposed to be, Leyna. A family.'

'I *have* family. I have parents who are King and Queen of a kingdom that needs them.'

So they don't have time for me to need them.

'And a grandmother whose heart is still broken from losing her husband almost ten years ago.'

And who's so focused on the crown she can't support the person who'll one day wear it.

'I have family, Xavier,' she repeated. 'What I *don't* have are friends. I need us to be friends.'

'You don't think we'd be friends if we were married?' His sombre tone told her things would probably change between them now, regardless of what she chose.

The panic inside her told her to make the right choice.

'We're best as friends. *Just* friends.'

'Is that you speaking, or your family?'

'It's me.' But a part of her wondered. 'I haven't listened to what they've said about us before. I don't care about that.'

'Then why are you so scared of what's between us, Leyna?' He closed the space between them with one step.

'Because...' She cleared her throat when her words came out more breathily than she wanted. 'Our lives aren't easy. The thing that's helped me through it is our friendship. We've been friends for almost twenty years.' Her voice broke. 'Don't take that away from me.'

He lifted her chin. 'I'm not taking anything away from you. I want to add to that friendship.' The left side of his mouth curved into a half-smile. 'Yes, we've been friends for twenty years. But you know I've been in love with you for most of that time.' She opened her mouth to dispute his words, but he shook his head. 'You know it's true.'

'No,' she said firmly.

'Really?' he drawled. 'Why have you been trying to stop me from saying it to you for all these years then?' His eyebrows lifted when she didn't reply, and then he nodded. 'Because you *do* know it. We both have from the moment I gave you that rose when we were five.'

When her heart melted at even the memory of it, she finally acknowledged the truth of his words. But he was right. She *was* scared. Scared of the change, and of what that change would mean for her life. One day she would be Queen of Aidara and she knew what that would demand from her.

And it wasn't because her grandmother had warned her of the demands of the role. Or the way she constantly referred to Xavier as a distraction, and their friendship as 'childish'. After years of defending what they had, Leyna had learnt to brush it off, knowing that Kathleen had a limited idea of what real relationships were.

No, Leyna's fears had nothing to do with Xavier, and everything to do with what she knew those demands would cost her. Because she'd seen exactly how they had affected her father.

King Clive had gone from exuberant Prince to reserved King. She had memories of her father being happy, chasing her around the royal gardens as her mother watched on, laughing. But in the ten years since he'd become King, that man had slowly faded away. Wrinkles of stress had replaced those of laughter. Every smile he gave her seemed like the hardest thing in the world.

The only remnant of the man her father used to be was the love he clearly still had for her mother. It made her ask, 'Will you still love me when I become Queen, when you become King, and we both have the hardest jobs in the world?'

'Of course I will.' His hand moved from her chin to brush away a stray curl. 'Who better to love and support you than someone who knows *exactly* what you're going through?'

'It's going to be harder than anything we've had to do so far, Xavier,' she said, to remind herself just as much as to remind him. 'You've seen what it's done to my father,' she whispered.

'We'll get through it,' Xavier said softly.

'What if we got through it better as just friends?'

'We've never been just friends, Leyna.'

'So why bring it all up now?'

'Because it's your birthday in two days. You'll be twenty-one and you'll be expected to marry. Just as I've been expected to marry for the last year.'

She pulled a lip between her teeth at the reminder of their one-year age difference.

'You know I've been waiting for you. It's the only reason I've managed to put my family off. I love you, Leyna. I want to be married to you. And I know that we'll be stronger together than we'll ever be apart. Apart here meaning *just* being friends.'

She smiled at that and felt the punishing pulse of fear ease. 'It's not as charming as you think, you know. Having all the answers.'

She saw the relief in his features, and he grinned. 'And yet you're still in love with me.'

'Full of yourself, too.'

'But you love me,' he insisted.

She studied him and felt a smile claim her lips. 'Since you seem so sure, I suppose I don't have to say it.'

'If you don't say it, I'll be forced to carry you back into that water.'

'And *I'll* be forced to decline your proposal.'

His eyes widened in mock fear. 'You *wouldn't.*'

'You have no idea what I'm capable of.'

'Show me.'

The teasing tone of his voice disappeared in a flash, and the light that had been in his eyes heated.

'Are you *propositioning*—'

She was silenced by his lips on hers.

It wasn't their first kiss—that had happened when they were thirteen and fourteen, beneath the very palm tree they stood under now. But it might as well have been their first. When they were barely teenagers, the kiss had been out of curiosity. It had been exploratory. As had the other kisses they'd shared since.

None of them compared to this.

It had the heat of a summer's day in Aidara. And the promise of passion that had been restrained for years. Leyna's arms were around Xavier's waist before she fully knew it, their bodies so close together she could feel every part of him. Her body responded and, for the first time in her life, Leyna felt like a woman. Not a daughter or a granddaughter. Certainly not like the heir to a throne.

No, she felt like a *woman*.

One who could make a man moan just as Xavier did now. One who had the power to make a man lift her from the ground and press her against the trunk of a tree so he could press even closer to her. She was lost in the sensation of his lips against hers, of his tongue in her mouth.

She was suddenly grateful they were at the beach, wearing the attire required by their location. It meant she didn't have to battle with clothing to feel the muscular planes of Xavier's body. It meant she could enjoy the way his hands touched—*claimed*—the curves of hers.

When his hand lifted a thigh so he could angle himself against her, Leyna heard a sound come from her throat. She felt Xavier still, and then he pulled his head away, just far enough so he could look into her eyes.

'What's wrong?'

'Nothing,' she breathed, and put a hand on the back of his neck, urging him closer.

'Leyna,' Xavier said. 'I've known you all my life. Tell me.'

'I just…' She felt her face burn. 'I've just never…'

'You know I haven't either.'

'I know,' she echoed, knowing that if Xavier had had another woman, she would have known about it. 'But…are we doing this now? Against a tree on a beach, with our bodyguards a short distance away?'

'I… I didn't think about that.'

Xavier took a deep breath, and then took a step back. Leyna immediately missed the contact.

'I didn't mean that we can't do it at all. I just… Well, I just pictured it on our wedding night. In a bed surrounded by candles and rose petals. With champagne cooling.'

She sounded like a fool. More so when silence followed her words. But then Xavier smiled.

'You *pictured* it?'

Her cheeks went hot, but she laughed. 'Maybe.'

'On our wedding night?'

Her heart softened at the emotion she heard in his voice. 'Yes.'

'So you always knew there was more, too?'

'Of course I did. Did you think I was resisting something I knew wasn't true?' She frowned. 'You were so sure…?'

'I was betting with the most important thing in my life, Leyna. I had to be.'

She stared at him, and then shook her head. 'If I didn't already love you, Xavier, I think I might have fallen for you right now.'

'But you do. Love me.'

'I do.' And, realising that he needed to hear the words, she said, 'I love you, Xavier.'

He pulled her into his arms and rested his forehead on hers. 'And you're going to marry me.'

'I am,' she answered, though it wasn't a question. 'As soon as I possibly can.'

'I think this might be—'

It happened so quickly that Leyna barely registered what had cut Xavier off. All she knew was that her royal aide, Carlos, was now standing in front of her and Xavier. Their bodyguards hovered just beyond him; their expressions were twisted with an emotion she couldn't read, but it had her heart pounding with fear.

'What is it?' she asked, stepping out of Xavier's embrace.

'I'm sorry to interrupt—' there was the briefest moment of hesitation before Carlos said '—Your Majesty.'

CHAPTER ONE

Ten years later

'IS HE HERE, CARLOS?'

'I'm afraid not, Your Majesty.'

For the second time in Leyna's life, Carlos had brought her news of the last thing she wanted to hear. Now, of course, he was bringing it to her as her private secretary and not as a royal aide.

But then, her father's death had changed more than just Carlos' title. She'd become Queen immediately, and had lost the only man she'd loved. And now the news that King Zacchaeus of Kirtida had not arrived for the State Banquet intended to affirm the Alliance of the Three Isles threatened to be just as life-changing.

She closed her eyes for the briefest moment and then nodded. Released a breath.

'Please find His Majesty, King Xavier, and ask him to join me in the library.'

'Of course, Your Majesty.'

When Carlos left, Leyna took another deep breath. And a moment to deal with the feelings tumbling through her stomach. She opened the doors to the balcony of her library and greedily inhaled the fresh air.

It felt like the only thing keeping her alive.

The panic came now. Not dull as it had been when she'd first heard that King Jaydon of Kirtida had been overthrown by his son, Zacchaeus. And nowhere near how it had felt when he'd consistently refused her and Xavier's attempts to discuss the future of the alliance binding their islands together, though she'd believed it sharp then.

No, the feeling cutting through her lungs now, tightening her throat and making her hands shake, was much worse.

But she only had a few moments before Carlos returned with Xavier. She forced herself to focus on her breathing, something she'd learnt to do when she'd taken over the crown after her father's death.

When her heart, broken from her breakup with Xavier and from her mother fleeing, had beat so hard she thought it would explode from her chest.

She straightened her spine when she heard the knock on the door, turning in time to see

Xavier stride past Carlos into the library. As it always did when she saw Xavier—despite the fact that their relationship now was only a political courtesy—her chest tightened.

She told her memories to stay where they belonged, but couldn't help the relief that washed through her at his presence.

'He's not here,' Xavier said immediately, and she tried not to wince at the tone.

'He's not. Which means—'

'That he is renouncing Kirtida's place in the Alliance of the Three Isles.'

'I'd like to think that isn't true. That Kirtida is still a part of our alliance.' She saw a glint in his blue—almost grey—eyes, and tilted her head. 'But his actions since he overthrew Jaydon speak volumes.'

'Refusing our calls to set up meetings *and* refusing to see us when we resorted to just arriving at Kirtida in hopes of a meeting?' Xavier asked gravely. 'Tonight was the last hope we had that he's willing to work with us, Leyna. So yes, I think his actions tell us exactly where we stand with him.'

'If we assume he'll withdraw—' panic rippled through her chest again '—what do we do?'

'We respond accordingly.'

'How?'

'We ensure that Zacchaeus knows the alliance between Aidara and Mattan is still intact. We ensure that our people know it, too.'

'I'm sure there isn't any doubt about that,' Leyna said. 'You *are* here at the dinner intended to do that very thing after all.'

'It isn't enough.'

She saw the determination in his eyes—in each of the once kind, now intimidating angles of his handsome face—and the relief she'd felt steadily ebbed. Her body tensed, and she saw that tension reflected in his tall, muscular frame, too.

'What do you have in mind?' she asked carefully.

'Something that will leave Zacchaeus and our people without any doubt about the strength of our alliance. Something that will reassure our people that Kirtida's absence from the Alliance of the Three Isles doesn't mean they are unprotected.'

Silence pulsed in the room, and then Leyna said, 'Tell me what you'd like us to do, Xavier.'

'We should get married.'

Leyna's thoughts immediately went back to that day on the beach when Xavier had proposed to her.

Her knees nearly buckled and she turned away from him and walked straight onto the balcony. She gripped the railing and fought for breath. And then she fought to be free of the memories.

They were vicious, she thought, and crept up on her when she least wanted them to. She'd only been fooling herself with her hope that they'd stay in the past. But she'd been desperate. Perhaps because she knew every moment she spent with Xavier would threaten to draw her back into what could have been.

She couldn't afford for that to happen. She couldn't afford to think about the hope, the love, that she'd felt on the day he'd proposed to her. If she did, she would inevitably think of the cold feeling that had come over her when Carlos had first called her 'Your Majesty'.

She would think about the days she'd spent in a daze of heartbreak, worsened by her mother leaving Aidara the moment they'd buried her father. She would remember the fear she'd felt about ruling alone. How all the warnings her grandmother had given her about Xavier had haunted her dreams.

And the utter devastation when she'd realised that she couldn't be the Queen Aidara needed with Xavier by her side.

She took a minute to compose herself. When she was sure the emotion and memories were as far away as she could push them, she walked back into the library. Xavier's face was stony, but just above his lip was a twitch Leyna recognised as anger.

'How would that work exactly? Us, married?'

'If we got married,' Xavier spoke in a careful tone, 'it would be clear—not only to Kirtida, but to the world—that Aidara and Mattan are united. And with our collective military, our resources, our people, we would be powerful enough to defend against anything Kirtida attempts.'

'Marriages end, Xavier,' she said in the same tone, and saw the heat of anger flare in his eyes.

Good.

'Royal marriages don't just *end*.'

'No,' she agreed. 'But you and I both know we can't anticipate what might happen in the future.'

Maybe bitterness spurred on her words, but she didn't give it much thought. Whatever motivated them didn't change that what she'd said was the truth. She'd seen it with her parents. Her father's death had made her mother forget her responsibilities to the crown. To Aidara. To her daughter.

Granted, Helene *had* married into the royal family of Aidara, and hadn't been Aidaraen herself. When Leyna was feeling sympathetic towards her mother, she thought it must have been hard for Helene to stay in the place where her heart had been broken.

But those times were rare, and quickly followed by the reminder that Helene had left her daughter to fend for herself in the hardest job in the world. Without any support.

'What does *that* mean?'

'It means exactly what I said. Marriages don't last for ever. You know that better than anyone.'

'Leave Erika out of this,' Xavier nearly growled, and Leyna's bitterness meshed with jealousy.

'You're the one bringing her into this,' she said lightly. Carefully. 'I wasn't talking about your marriage—I meant the institution, not your spouse.'

She gave him time to process—though, if she were honest with herself, it was more for *her* to find her own control again.

'What are you suggesting, Leyna?'

'Only that marriage is not enough to secure an alliance. Especially a precarious one.'

'So what do you want then? A child?' he asked sarcastically.

She'd had a nippy reply on the tip of her tongue that disappeared the moment her mind processed his words. There was something in that, she thought. But, for the life of her, she couldn't wade through the flood of emotions his suggestion had released to identify what that something was.

But, because she had to, she struggled through it. Through the hope that came from a dream she'd given up on a long time ago. Of being a family with Xavier. Of having children with him.

Through the sadness that had come with the realisation that that would never happen. Through the resentment that she would still have to carry a child—with some man who would be her husband though she would never love him—for the sake of the crown.

And again, through the resentment that she'd given up her dreams for the crown.

And then again, through the hope that maybe duty would make that dream come true after all.

'It's not a real option,' Xavier interrupted her thoughts. Her gaze moved to his and held, sparks she would never admit aloud still flying between them.

'Unless it is.'

'How would that possibly improve the situation with Zacchaeus?'

'For the reasons you outlined. Except now

we don't only have the marriage backing our alliance, but a child as well. Which would mean that even if something happens to one of us, Aidara and Mattan would still be protected by the other.'

'Mattan would take care of Aidara if anything happened to you,' Xavier answered stiffly.

'Even if that's true, whoever I marry would need to give me a child. An heir to the Aidaraen throne. You know that,' she told him, and saw the confirmation of it in his eyes. 'The same goes for you. There'll need to be a child for the Mattanian throne, too. And you can't deny the political power in having one child as an heir to both kingdoms' thrones.'

Xavier ran a hand through his dark hair, giving her a glimpse of the lighter streaks that she knew showed when it wasn't styled so precisely. It made the colour of his skin, which spoke of the mixed African and European heritage they both had, look like a tan. As though he had lazily picked one up on holiday instead of from the work he did amongst his citizens.

But anyone who knew Xavier couldn't deny he was a king. Leyna had always thought he looked exactly as a king should—authoritative, uncompromising, powerful. Only she had been privy to the other side of him when they'd been growing up. The easy, laidback man who'd relaxed on the beach with her and would casually hold her hand as they walked through the gardens.

It felt like a punishment that she no longer saw that Xavier. No, now she, too, experienced only that authoritative, uncompromising and powerful side of *King* Xavier.

Just as everyone else did.

But could she blame him?

'Let me see if I understand this,' Xavier said. 'You think that if we marry it won't be enough to strengthen the alliance between Aidara and Mattan on the off-chance something might happen to one of us. So you want to have a child to make sure that *if* something happens, our kingdoms will still be protected because there is a single heir to both our thrones?'

'Yes,' she answered. 'And don't be so dismissive of the possibility of something happening to one of us. We've both seen people we love die younger than they should have. It *is* a possibility.' She gave him a chance to process before continuing. 'A child gives us assurances in both cases. If something happens and if it doesn't, because there's no way Kirtida can misinterpret marriage and an heir.

There's also no better way to strengthen the alliance.'

'That might be true, except for one little thing.'

'What?'

'I can't give you a child.'

CHAPTER TWO

XAVIER WATCHED THE shock in her eyes disappear behind the curtain that hid all her emotions. The emotions he'd once been able to read as easily as he did his favourite books.

'What does that mean?' Leyna asked softly. He wanted to tell her—would have, had it been ten years before—but he couldn't bring himself to say that he was infertile. The fact that he'd alluded to it at all told him how much she shook him.

And how much he wanted to shake *her*.

How much he wanted to crack that perfectly logical, reasonable veneer she wore like a shield.

'It means there are cracks in that perfect plan of yours. And it's all a little…desperate.'

'*You* were the one who brought it up,' she shot back, reminding him of yet another of his slips. 'And yes, a child is desperate, but aren't we in a desperate situation?'

'So, you're saying desperate times call for desperate measures?'

'If you'd like to use that cliché to help you understand it, then yes.'

'And how would we conceive this child?' He knew he wasn't asking it because of his fertility problems but, again, because he found himself wanting to pierce through that cold facade. 'Should I stay after the banquet for us to get…reacquainted?'

He hated how bitter he sounded—worse still, how the bitterness had made him more vulgar than he'd intended. He watched her honey-coloured skin go pale, and felt the satisfaction of it just as acutely as he felt the shame.

Her lack of colour made the golden-brown of her hair—the green of her eyes—all the more striking. And if he added the gold dress she wore, which clung to her curves in a way that made him forget she was a queen…

She wasn't the delicate Princess from their youth any more, he thought. Though her face still had its slight angles and there were still freckles lightly spread over her nose, the woman who had laughed with him in the waters that separated their islands—the woman who'd once agreed to marry him—was gone.

The woman who stood in front of him now had a realism in her eyes that sent an ache

through his body. The light that had always
been there had been dimmed by whatever she'd
gone through in the ten years since they'd been
close. There was power, more authority, too.
She'd changed, he knew.

But then, so had he.

'It won't work,' she told him, colour flooding her skin again. 'I know you're trying to
shake me, but it won't work.'

'Won't it?' he asked, taking a step towards
her. Her eyes widened, and awareness sizzled
through his body. He'd loved those eyes once.
They'd told him everything he needed to know.
And though there were many less disturbing
memories to choose from, his mind offered
him the day Leyna had agreed to marry him.

Her eyes had shone with a love he hadn't
thought capable of hurting him the way it—the
way *she*—had. And then there had been the
desire in her eyes a few moments later. When
he'd had her against a tree. She'd wanted him
as much as he'd wanted her, but there had been
fear, uncertainty, too.

He saw those emotions in her eyes again
now. And it made him wonder whether they
were caused by the same reason. That she'd
never been with a man before. The thought
stirred a mess of emotions in his chest that he
didn't want to think about. Though there *was*

one thing he couldn't ignore, and that was the fact that he still wanted her, regardless of what the answer to that question was.

It shocked him into stepping back.

'No, it won't,' she said, and he heard the breathiness she tried to mask. 'Because we both have kingdoms to think about. Unless you've forgotten that's the real reason for all of this?'

She was right, he thought. He needed to think about his kingdom. And that meant he couldn't deny her suggestion had merit. If he pushed all his feelings about it aside, he could recognise the strength and subsequent protection a marriage and child would offer Mattan.

He was also sure his family would approve. Sure, they'd treated his relationship with Leyna as an indulgence in the past. Mostly because they couldn't deny how beneficial a union between him and Leyna—between Mattan and Aidara—would have been. But the moment they'd realised that wouldn't be happening, they'd told him to snap out of it. To think of his kingdom.

Since that was what drove him now, too, he knew they would approve. And since the man he and Leyna had grown up with no longer seemed to exist in Zacchaeus, Xavier was forced to face that this might be their only option.

Which meant he needed to tell her the truth of his fertility problems.

The thought had him heading straight to the alcohol decanter next to her desk. He flipped over two glasses, and poured a splash of the brown liquid into each. He offered her one and, when she took it, downed his own. He would have liked another, but that wouldn't have been wise considering what he was in Aidara to do. Or what he was about to say.

'I can't have children.'

He set the glass back in its tray. It gave him a reason to avoid the emotion on her face.

'You…' Her voice faded. 'I'm so sorry, Xavier.'

'I've accepted it.'

'How…how do you know?'

'I was married, Leyna,' he reminded her, and saw hurt pass over her face so quickly he didn't know what to think about it. So he continued. 'Erika and I tried to have children before she died. We could never conceive.'

'That must have been terrible for you…and Erika. I'm sorry.'

Emotion churned inside him. Erika had been devastated by their battle to have children. And when they'd found out that there was no medical reason why they couldn't, she'd turned angry.

By then, she'd learnt that the allure of marrying a king had only been in her imagination.

That the reality of it was far more demand-ing—and sometimes more demeaning—than she'd wanted.

Would she still have felt the same if she'd become a mother?

He never gave himself the permission to consider it. All he knew was that the only thing that had kept Erika committed to being Queen had been the prospect of a child. And when that hadn't happened she had become more and more withdrawn. And he'd felt more and more guilty. Because though there'd been no proof that it was him, it *had* to be.

'Why not? Why can't you have children?' Leyna's soft voice interrupted his thoughts.

'We tried and we didn't conceive.'

'Yes, you said that.' She frowned. 'That doesn't mean *you* were the reason you couldn't conceive.'

'It wasn't Erika's fault,' he said sharply.

'I wasn't saying that it was. But there *is* such a thing as unexplained infertility.'

It was what the doctor had told them, too. But, as someone who'd needed answers, Xavier hadn't been happy with that. Neither had Erika. So he'd accepted the blame for it.

'So there's no medical reason that you can't conceive?'

He clenched his jaw. 'No.'

'Then we still have a chance.'

'I must have missed this unfeeling side of you when we were friends.'

He saw her flinch, but her voice was steady. 'The reality of our lives—of our *duty*—doesn't always allow us to feel, Xavier.'

'Is that how we'll conceive this child then? Without feeling?'

'Why not?'

'You have to have *some* kind of feeling to conceive a child, Leyna.'

'Perhaps, if you want to do it naturally.' She raised an eyebrow—taunting him, he knew, with the insinuation. 'But, since this is going to be a contract, I think we should consider other options. To keep things…official.'

Relief and disappointment mingled in his chest. 'You mean artificial insemination?'

'Or IVF.'

'It would take time we might not have.'

'Which is why we should do it as soon as possible.'

With each word, his heart grew heavier. It weighed down his response so that, although he knew she was right, he couldn't bring himself to agree. Agreeing would mean that the distance he'd sought from her for ten years would be destroyed. It would bring back all the feelings he'd avoided thinking about since

Erika had died. Feelings of failure, of heart-break.

And if he agreed to marry Leyna he knew he would feel as though he was being disloyal to Erika. Worse still, if it worked and Leyna fell pregnant, he would feel as though he'd *betrayed* Erika. He'd be living the life she'd once accused him of always wanting.

He wasn't sure he could live with that guilt.

'Do you agree, Xavier?'

'Does it matter? You seem to have every-thing neatly planned anyway.'

'Neatly?' she repeated, disbelief in her voice. 'This is probably the least neat thing I've ever planned, Xavier. Do you think I want to be married to you, to carry your *child*?'

'Well, if it's such a burden then—'

'Stop it,' she snapped, anger turning her cheeks red. 'Our lives are filled with burdens. They're called responsibilities. They're a part of our duty.' He saw her chest heave, revealing the passion with which she spoke her words. 'Duty comes first, Xavier. It always has and it always will. This plan I've so *neatly* outlined is going to require sacrifices from the both of us, and it won't be pleasant. In fact, I'm pretty sure it might destroy me.'

Her eyes widened and she turned away from him. It had been her first real show of emotion—proper, spontaneous emotion that told him the veneer of aloofness had been cracked. It had surprised her and, though he'd wanted to crack that shield, it had surprised *him*, too.

He didn't know what to make of her words. *What* would destroy her? Working with him? Being married to him? Carrying his child? Was she just as affected as he was by the prospect that this decision would make them share their lives in the way they'd always imagined? Or was it because the circumstances of this life together were nothing like they'd imagined, ensuring that this decision would make their lives infinitely more complicated?

'Perhaps there's a simpler solution,' he said suddenly, his thoughts turning him desperate.

'There is no simple solution for us. For this,' she said, turning back to him. Her eyes were bright, troubled, and he wanted to reach out and comfort her. But he didn't. Of course he didn't. He didn't know her any more. Comforting her wasn't his job.

'Duty is never simple,' he said mockingly. But she responded seriously.

'No, it isn't. It will never be simple for us, nor will it ever be simple between us.'

It was the first time she'd made any kind of mention of their past, and he wasn't sure how he felt about it. So he didn't respond, instead letting the silence stretch. He felt it build, felt the tension pulse from both of them.

It made him want to ask her why she'd done it. Why she'd broken his heart. Why she'd broken *them*. It made him want to tell her how long he'd been broken. How he'd still had to pick up the pieces in the first years of his marriage to Erika. How that had started the cracks that had eventually broken him and Erika, too.

'We can try to set up a meeting with Zacchaeus one more time,' she said, breaking the silence.

'You know that won't work.'

'Then we move onto Plan B.'

'Marriage and a child?'

'Marriage and a child,' she confirmed.

'We don't have the luxury of time here,' Xavier said quietly. 'If Zacchaeus decides to attack either of us, our kingdoms will be helpless to stop him.'

'One more attempt at diplomacy, and then we move onto Plan B, Xavier,' Leyna said again. 'Now, we should get back before they realise we're gone.'

She set the glass down, its contents untouched, and walked out of the room before he could reply.

CHAPTER THREE

LEYNA HAD HAD to leave the room—to escape Xavier's company before she said something she regretted.

She already regretted too much of that conversation. That burst of emotion had reminded her of the woman she'd once been. The woman who'd died long ago. She needed to remind herself that the Leyna who'd let emotion guide her was gone. She *had* to be led by logic and reason. By the needs of her kingdom.

Because she was terrified of what would happen to her—*inside* of her—if she didn't.

Her steps faltered. Her heart stuttered. Hurt pushed at the wall she'd hidden it behind. She closed her eyes, gave herself a moment. And then she straightened her shoulders and pushed ahead, forcing it all out of her mind as she walked into the hall.

Her royal duties required her attention.

Each year one of the islands in the Alliance

of the Three Isles hosted the State Banquet to affirm their ties with other countries. There were thirty dignitaries there that evening and, considering the Isles' geographical location, many of them were from Africa. The others were European, who, in honour of the three British men who'd found the islands with their African wives at the end of the eighteenth century, kept their ties with the Isles.

Leyna mingled, moving from the King of Spain to the King of Swaziland, and then to the delegation from South Africa. Before she knew it, dinner had been announced. She walked to the head of the table, her stomach turning when she saw Xavier. It wasn't a surprise— it was custom that the monarchs of the Isles sit there—so she forced her feelings at seeing his blank expression aside and thought again of her duty.

She touched Xavier's arm before he could take his seat.

'We can't have an empty seat at the head of the table. It would make Zacchaeus' absence more conspicuous, and I won't be able to field questions as easily if it's staring our guests in the face. Someone has to sit in Kirtida's place.'

He frowned down at her, but nodded. 'Aidaraen?'

She shook her head. 'My grandmother is the

only one from Aidara who would be appropriate, and she—' *She no longer seems to think
she needs to support her kingdom when she
doesn't approve of its queen.* 'She isn't here.
Can you ask someone from your family?'

'My grandmother,' he said immediately, but
she could sense his reluctance. So things hadn't
got better in the ten years they'd grown apart,
she thought. 'She'd be the best option, considering my mother couldn't be here tonight.' His
mother was ill, Leyna remembered. 'Please
excuse me.'

Formality—distance—lined his words. But
it was for the best, she told herself, and hated
the ache in her chest that said otherwise.

A few minutes later, Xavier returned with a
graceful older woman at his side. Envy slith-
ered its way through her before she shook it
off. It was natural to envy the grace and poise
the former Queen Consort of Mattan carried
effortlessly with her. But envy was not a trait
Leyna wanted to have as a queen, nor as a
woman.

'Your Majesty,' Leyna said and curtsied.

'Let's not waste time with the formalities,
Leyna.' Xavier's grandmother brushed kisses
on both Leyna's cheeks, and Leyna found her
lips curving.

'It's lovely to see you, ma'am.'

The older woman sighed. 'I recall you using that term years ago. But perhaps now we've reached the point where we can both use each other's first names. Paulina will do. And don't you dare refuse.'

Paulina lifted a hand to wave off Leyna's response, and Leyna nodded.

'As you wish… Paulina.'

Though she got an approving smile from Paulina, the name felt wrong on Leyna's lips. To deal with it, Leyna made a point of avoiding addressing Paulina by name. She received a few looks that told her Paulina knew what she was doing, but Leyna just smiled in return and moved onto the next topic. Conversations were easy for her. Except when they were with former best friends—*fiancés*—Leyna considered, her eyes flitting over Xavier.

'I'd hoped to see the new King of Kirtida here with us tonight,' Paulina said when things were loud enough at the table that no one would overhear.

Though she could hardly manage to forget it, Leyna winced at the reminder. 'I had, too.'

'We should have anticipated this mess,' Paulina continued. 'There was always something in that boy's eyes.'

Leyna didn't respond, and Paulina turned her attention to the conversation beside her. Leyna was grateful. Her thoughts had clamoured at Paulina's words, and she told herself, very deliberately, that it didn't make her any less of a queen that she *hadn't* anticipated their current situation.

It didn't mean she'd failed her people.

She lived with the constant fear that she wasn't doing enough. It didn't matter how hard she worked, that fear remained. And she'd worked *hard*. She'd had to rebuild the morale of a kingdom that had lost its King and Queen in a matter of weeks. She'd had to earn their trust and make them believe that, though she was only twenty-one, she *could* be their Queen.

It had required all her time and all her attention. It had reminded her of her grandmother's warnings. Was it any wonder she hadn't had time for Xavier any more? She'd broken things off the minute she'd realised—*really* realised—how much work she had ahead of her.

It had hurt her to do so—more still when the demands of *his* crown hadn't kept him from having a life. From having a relationship.

With someone who wasn't her.

She closed her eyes against the anger, the jealousy, the resentment and *pain,* and fought off the loneliness that threatened to creep in. As it did almost every day.

'Stop frowning,' Xavier said under his breath. 'People will think there's something wrong with the food.'

'Not the food, just the alliance they're all here to celebrate.'

'Don't,' he warned. 'We'll talk about it later.'

'Yes, sir.'

She looked over in surprise when she heard his fork scrape against the plate. He was holding his utensils so tightly that his knuckles were white. It had her heart racing, especially since she wasn't sure what had upset him.

'Relax,' she said lightly. 'We have to keep the illusion of peace between the two of us.'

'Are we at war then?'

'No,' she answered truthfully. 'But our lives might end up being the collateral to stave one off.'

He didn't respond to that, and somehow they made it through the rest of the dinner without saying another word to each other. Leyna led her guests to the more casual State Hall where the speeches would take place and gifts would be exchanged. She stood at the front next to the royal family of Mattan—Paulina, Xavier, his sister, Alika, with her husband, and his other sister, Nalini—accepting gifts with a smile even though she knew she was being watched.

No, she thought when her spine went rigid.

She wasn't being watched so much as *judged*. She knew her guests were wondering where the other member of Aidara's royal family was. They'd always wanted that show of unity, especially after her mother had left Aidara. It seemed to reassure her people and their allies that Aidara was still as strong as it had been when Leyna's grandfather, her grandmother Kathleen's husband, had ruled.

But the last time Leyna had refused a suitor Kathleen had brought before her, her grandmother had declared that Leyna was a lost cause and had left Aidara for a diplomatic trip to South Africa.

It spoke volumes to Leyna that that was the least of her problems now. Because she also knew her guests were speculating more about the absence of the royal family of Kirtida than they were about Kathleen.

Murmurs had spread through the room as they'd gone through the formalities of the gift exchanges. No doubt discussing what the implications of Kirtida's absence would be. She'd soothed many of the concerns when she'd done her rounds earlier, but that wouldn't stop the rumours.

And there was nothing she could do about that.

She felt the room snap to attention before she

saw why, and then felt her own body straighten in anticipation of the speech Xavier would be giving on behalf of the Isles. He'd stepped in front of the small podium that had been designed for the occasion. It was his presence, she thought. It commanded attention. She admired it.

He carried it with him so effortlessly—the authority, the confidence—that no one would have suspected he'd once begged Leyna not to leave him.

'You'd never know how broken he is, would you?'

Leyna frowned, wondering how someone had read her thoughts. She shook it off and glanced over to see Xavier's sister Nalini now standing beside her.

'What do you mean?'

'What do you see when you look at my brother?'

Leyna's eyes shifted to Xavier. His muscular body wore the uniform representing his kingdom with ease, his handsome features set in an expression that was both commanding and open. Her heart fluttered, and she blushed when she saw Nalini watching her.

'I see a king.'

Nalini took a few seconds to respond. 'I think that's who he sees, too. I think that's the *only* thing he sees. He lost the man somewhere. I think maybe it was when he lost the woman he loved.'

'I can only imagine what he must have gone through when Erika died. Losing someone you love is difficult.'

'That *was* hard, of course,' Nalini agreed. 'But I was actually talking about you.'

Shock seized her tongue, and there was a long pause before Leyna replied.

'No. I mean, he didn't… I don't think that's true.'

'Oh, it's true,' Nalini assured her, uncharacteristically serious. 'Things became worse after Erika. But it started with you.'

Leyna had no response to that.

'Xavier's marriage wasn't…easy, Leyna. And then they struggled to have a baby, and… Well, it was a heavy burden on Xavier. Worse because Erika didn't know how to carry her part of that burden—of being Queen *and* of not conceiving naturally.'

Leyna felt as if she were being sucked into quicksand. She drew on her breathing techniques, knowing that she had to control the panic building in her chest.

'He loved her and he was devastated when she passed on. But it's been three years now and…' Nalini's voice faded and Leyna could see the Princess's concern for her brother.

'Why are you telling me this?'

'Not to upset you,' Nalini said quickly. 'I'm sorry if I have.' Leyna nodded, but didn't speak. 'I think… I'd *hoped* that you'd help him. I know that's probably out of line, but you're the only person…' She trailed off and then took a breath. 'I'm telling you this because I thought you'd be able to remind him of the person he used to be. The man who'd *lived* and didn't just rule.'

Leyna barely noticed that Xavier had finished his speech, but her heart raced when she caught him walking towards them.

'Please,' Nalini whispered, and Leyna didn't get the chance to respond when Xavier joined them.

'That wasn't incredibly boring,' Nalini said brightly. Perhaps *too* brightly, Leyna thought.

'Thank you, I think?' But he frowned, looking at Nalini and then Leyna. It took Leyna a second to realise that she should say something to him, too, and she cleared her throat.

'It was wonderful, thank you. I hope my speech next year is just as elegant when Mattan hosts the banquet.'

'Are you okay?'

'Yes,' she answered quickly, and avoided

Nalini's eyes. 'Please excuse me. I think Carlos is looking for me.'

He wasn't doing anything to indicate that he was, but Leyna strode towards him with enough purpose that anyone watching would think he *had* called for her. When he saw her coming, his eyes widened and he stood at attention.

'Your Majesty.'

'You can relax, Carlos. I just need an excuse to get some air.'

She gave him a shaky smile and saw some of the tension seep from his stance.

'Would you buy me some time? Tell anyone who's looking for me I'm speaking with someone else privately. You can do that until I return. I won't be long.'

Though she read confusion in his eyes, Carlos nodded and Leyna made her way through the secret tunnels that led to Aidara's private beach. She kicked off her shoes at the edge of the sand and lifted the hem of her dress. It was practical—she wanted to be able to walk more easily—but she also didn't want to ruin the beautiful dress. Then she stopped just before the water reached her feet and took a long steadying breath.

This beach held so many memories for her. Despite the fact that those memories were tainted with sadness now, it was still the place she came to for calm. For balance. She needed both now as the information Nalini had told her swirled in her head.

Xavier had had a difficult marriage. The knowledge grieved her. Even though she'd felt betrayed when he'd moved on so quickly from her, Leyna hadn't wanted him to be unhappy. She'd wanted him to find contentment. To live a full life without her.

No, she corrected herself. What she'd wanted was for him to live a happy, full life *with* her. It was a contradiction that Nalini's words had alerted Leyna to. She had never wanted Xavier to be unhappy but, if she was honest with herself, she didn't want him to be happy without her.

She was a selfish, *selfish* person.

And now she was planning a marriage with him. And a *child*.

Hadn't she *jumped* on that? She hadn't wasted time thinking about what being married to him, what carrying his child would cost her. Not until she'd admitted to him that it might just destroy her.

She hadn't *wanted* to admit it, but she couldn't deny the truth of it now. She'd worked even harder rebuilding *herself* than she had on rebuilding her kingdom ten years ago. Turning away from Xavier had been absolutely soul-destroying. The only way she'd been able to survive the decision since was to focus on her duty. To focus on what she'd turned away from Xavier for.

She'd refused her grandmother's suitors, had refused to date since. Hell, she'd refused to make time for *any* emotion that wasn't necessary to run her kingdom. And now, with the possibility of a future with Xavier looming… It was enough for all the emotions she'd been ignoring to come flooding back in.

Leyna could see herself carrying a baby that was part her, part Xavier. She could already feel it move inside her, and see herself holding it for the first time. It would have Xavier's almost grey eyes and her brown curly hair. It would have his laugh…

'You can't keep abandoning your guests like this, Leyna.'

She whirled around at Xavier's voice, wondering for the briefest of moments if she'd imagined it. But he was there, walking towards her, his bare feet a stark contrast to the full-dress uniform he wore.

'I just needed a break to think.'

'About?'

She let out a strangled laugh. 'What do you think?'

'I think you need to put duty first. Doing

that means marriage. And, apparently, a child,' he added, and her heart thudded.

'Easier said than done,' she told him, and turned back just in time to see the water splash millimetres from her feet.

'The conundrum of duty.'

'You say that like it's affected your life somehow.'

'That's a joke, right?'

'I don't mean in the usual sense.' Her eyes followed the waves as they pulled back before crashing at the shore again. 'I mean, how has it changed your life? How has it *dictated* your life?'

'You really want to know?' he asked, his voice low, tinged with something that had her turning towards him. A poor decision, she thought immediately, when she saw the look on his face—when she saw the seriousness, the fire, in his eyes.

Her belly stirred with a desire long-forgotten, her heart reminding her that they were in *their* place. That the reason he'd been able to find her when no one else would have was because he knew this was where she'd come to think. Where he'd found her countless times before.

Suddenly, the sound of the waves provided an alluring backing track. The night-time sky with its moonlight and stars offered more romance than she wanted.

She took a step back. 'Tell me.'

'Why don't you go first?'

'What is this? I show you mine, you show me yours?'

'No.' He took a step towards her now, and her heart pounded even harder as her body tightened. 'But something tells me that your experiences are the reason for mine.'

CHAPTER FOUR

'THERE YOU GO AGAIN,' Leyna said hoarsely. 'Thinking you have all the answers.'

'Not all of them,' he replied, his hand lifting before he could stop it to brush at a curl that had escaped from her bun. 'Just this one.'

He knew he was playing with fire. The beach, that dress, the magnetism she exuded without even trying… It was bound to get him burned, and he still had the scars from the last time he'd played with the fire.

Yet he couldn't move away.

'I've made too many decisions for duty,' she said softly. 'I can't possibly begin to name them all.'

'How about the night you told me you couldn't be with me? When you said that you'd mistaken the love you felt for me *as a friend* for more?' Forgotten anger stirred and his hand moved to the small of her back, pressing her closer to him. 'I *begged* you to tell me what was happening, to help you get through whatever it was.'

'I told you the truth then.' Her voice shook. 'There was never more. There *couldn't* be more.'

'You're saying there isn't more, Leyna?' He dipped his head so their mouths were a breath apart. 'What royal duty had you deciding you couldn't be with me?'

'Stop it,' she said, and tried to put distance between them. But he kept his hand on her back, refusing to allow her to pull away from him again. 'Xavier, let me go.'

Her voice had gone cold. The shield was back up, he realised. His hand loosened its grip on her and he slipped it into his pocket and took a step back. His fingers curled into a fist when he realised his hand was now shaking, and he took another step away from her.

She was making him lose his mind. His bearings. And if he didn't have them, what would stop him from continuing where they'd left off ten years ago?

It was the talk of marriage and children—as though it were as easy as it had been then— that had made him forget about the life he'd lived in those ten years since. He could almost hear Erika's voice mocking him, asking him whether she was really so easy to forget. Taunting him that things were turning out exactly as he'd wanted them to all along.

It had been a constant argument between them. No matter how much Xavier had told her he was committed to *them*, that Leyna had no part in *their* relationship, the argument had remained. And no matter how hard he had fought to keep Leyna separate from his life with Erika, she was always there. In the simplest things, and the most complicated emotions.

Erika had deserved more. She hadn't deserved to be compared to another woman. Didn't he know what it was like to be compared to someone who'd come before? To be held to an unfair standard? It didn't matter who that person was, the feeling was terrible. And his wife had deserved more than that. She'd deserved more than a sudden death when she was barely thirty, too.

He hadn't been able to give her all that she'd deserved when she was alive, but he could try to make up for that now. And what she deserved now—what her memory deserved—was that he keep things between him and Leyna strictly professional.

His kingdom deserved it, too. He could still hear the words his father had said to him after Leyna had broken up with him. Xavier had been so heartbroken he hadn't been able to keep up with his responsibilities. His father had taken him aside, and had given him the tough love he'd needed.

Always put the kingdom first.

He might not have a choice about what they had to do to protect their kingdoms, but he could choose to remember that. To honour his kingdom and his wife. To set boundaries where Leyna was concerned. Yes, he could do *that*.

'We'll have to make the people believe it,' he said. If she was confused—or relieved—by the shift in topic, she didn't show it.

'I don't think it matters whether they believe it. They'll appreciate our attempts to protect them.'

'They probably will. But they'd know why, and it might have them panicking. If we do this, it will speak to their desire to believe that everything is fine.'

'I suppose that's true,' she said, and shifted the hem of her dress from her left hand to her right. It drew his attention to her long, shapely legs, and he looked away before they tempted his already tenuous control. 'We should head back.'

He walked with her but said, 'We should talk about this more.'

'I agree. Tomorrow? We can meet here

again, if that suits you, and talk through the details. Xavier?' she said when they reached the pathway leading back to the castle. 'Are we really doing this? Getting married and having a child?'

'We have to.'

She nodded. 'I suppose there's a wedding and a baby in our future then.'

'For the sake of our kingdoms.'

He said it as a reminder to both of them of what was at stake. They had to put their feelings aside and focus on protecting their kingdoms.

She straightened her shoulders, an expression fierce with determination on her face, and repeated, 'For the sake of our kingdoms.'

Xavier made his way to the roof of the Aidaraen castle, more than a little annoyed that Leyna was there when she should have been in her library, preparing for their meeting together. They'd agreed the previous evening to hash out the details of their arrangement there. And, since it was something neither of them really wanted to do, the least Leyna could have done was to make sure she kept to their plan.

As he climbed the stairs, though, he realised that he should be glad she wasn't at the beach.

He'd struggled with the memories when they'd been there together the night before. In the clear light of day—after the sleepless hours he'd spent thinking about it—he knew that seeing her in the place that had always been theirs had been partly responsible for the spell that had taken over him.

The other parts he didn't care to think about. But, since he'd made a pact with himself the night before, it didn't matter anyway.

The more he thought about it, the more he realised the roof of the castle was the perfect venue for the type of conversation they needed to have. Private, secure. But his thoughts stalled when he walked through the door.

The usually empty space now held a round table in the middle of it. The table was set for an intimate date, with red and pink flowers in the centre and an ice-bucket with champagne cooling just beside it. Each corner of the rooftop held a potted tree and colourful plants, green and bright, as though they'd been there since the beginning of time.

His eyes then moved to the woman who stood beside the table, and his gut tightened.

Leyna wore a simple white dress that was cut in a V at her neck and flowed gracefully down to her ankles. It was perfectly respectable. Or it would have been, he thought, if it had been on anyone else.

On her, the demure dress looked as if it was designed to be torn off. Thrown aside by hands—*his* hands—in order to roam over the slim curves of her body as his lips took hers, his tongue tasting whether she was still as innocent as she'd been when he'd first kissed her at fourteen, or as alluring—as *seductive*—as she'd been the day she'd said yes to his proposal.

He clenched his fists and though he knew he ought to make his way to her, he moved back. It was a futile attempt to distance himself from the memories. From the attraction. From the consuming need his body ached with when he saw her, tempting him to suggest they try for a child the natural way.

Why was it so difficult to ignore? He had the best reasons not to want her. She'd broken his heart, damn it, and trampled on its pieces when she'd walked out of his life. He'd even promised *himself* that he would try harder. For his kingdom. For Erika.

He had the best reasons, he thought again, and still they didn't seem to be enough. Not when he had a compelling reason for them not to be.

He took in the classically beautiful features

of her face, framed by tendrils of golden-brown curls. The rest of her hair was tied at the top of her head, almost making a crown, he thought. The casual style seemed no less royal than the elegant, swept back one she'd worn the night before.

She was still as captivating, as *breathtaking* as she'd been when he'd first fallen in love with her. And damn her for it.

'What's all this?' Xavier said, refusing to wince when he heard the sharpness in his voice.

'Well, you said we need to make our kingdoms believe this,' she said mildly. 'There'll be a helicopter flying over the castle in about thirty minutes. They'll take pictures, which will accompany an article suggesting we've been seeing each other in secret for the past month.'

It was clever, he thought, but didn't say so. 'You think one month will be enough?'

'They've always shipped us together, even when we weren't.' She lifted a shoulder and then dropped it gracefully. 'It'll say a month but they'll believe it to be longer. I think it will work.'

He nodded, and looked at the table in front of them. 'I assume there'll be some sort of meal involved with this.'

'Yes.' She nodded at a man who had somehow known to appear behind him at the appropriate moment. 'We can take a seat in the meantime.'

They were alone on the roof—a rarity for both of them, he knew. It indicated the privacy they had there, especially as he was sure their guards had every possible entry covered. He pulled her seat out for her and then took his own. And wondered how their solitude would affect the lascivious thoughts he'd been having about her.

'There have to be rules with this,' Leyna started.

'Well, first, we have to decide what *this* is.'

'I thought we already had. We're getting married. Having a child.'

They were words that had been repeated so often in the last twenty-four hours he thought he'd remember them for the rest of his life. Just as he would the determination covering the hesitance in her tone.

'Yes. But *when* will we get married? *When* will we have the child? Will it be a big, flashy wedding? Will we use IVF or IUI? And when we announce all of this, what will we do about Zacchaeus?'

'I get your point,' she said. 'So let's get to the details then. First, though, I want to say that I reached out to Zacchaeus again this morning.'

'So did I.'

Her lips curved slightly. 'Great minds. I'm assuming you got the same response I did?'

'You mean no response?'

She nodded. 'We've tried to resolve this diplomatically. Now we move on.'

'Let's talk about the wedding first. When?'

'We'll need at least a month to plan a proper wedding. Two or three if we'd like to have our international allies attend.'

'That might be too long,' he said. 'The situation with Zacchaeus is a ticking bomb that could go off at any moment.'

'I agree, but I don't think we'd get away with a rushed wedding. Not if we want to assure everyone that the alliance is intact and will thrive because of our marriage.'

'We can't just wait around for Zacchaeus to decide to make a move.'

'I know.' Her fingers tapped lightly on a champagne glass. 'What happened to him? Zacchaeus, I mean. He was quiet, yes, and perhaps even a little one-sided and angry. But he was never malicious. Not like this.'

'I thought the same thing when I heard about the coup. I heard…' He trailed off, shook his head. 'It's all speculation. Not worth mentioning.'

'Well, you've mentioned it now. You might as well tell me.'

He almost smiled. 'I heard that Jaydon had fallen ill, and Zacchaeus overthrowing him had been a way to save face.'

'That can't possibly be true. Why would either of them have to save face because of an illness?'

'Which is exactly why I didn't think it would be worth mentioning. There's another possible explanation for all of this, so we have to act.' He waited for the food to be served, and when they were alone again continued. 'What if we announced our wedding at the end of this week?'

'It *would* send a clear message about our intentions,' she considered. 'But the end of this week might be too soon if—' She broke off and her cheeks went pink.

'If what?'

She straightened her spine. 'I saw my doctor this morning. After our discussion, I wanted to be proactive so—' the pink darkened '—I spoke to him about what it would mean for us to do IVF or IUI.'

His heart beat faster but he only raised his eyebrows. 'Busy morning for you.'

'You just said we didn't have the luxury of time with this situation,' she said defensively. 'And I knew the process could include medication and…' She sighed. 'Why am I defending this? It's something we have to do. So, would you like to hear what he said or not?'

'I already know what he said,' Xavier replied. He thought about all the doctor's appointments he and Erika had had. How, after each of them, he'd felt her shrink into herself. How, after several rounds of IUI which had failed, when they'd finally decided on IVF, she'd had an aneurism before they could do the embryo transfer.

'Our options are IUI or IVF,' he said almost mechanically. 'IUI might be our best option considering our time constraints, depending on where you are in your cycle.'

'Yes,' she answered, looking taken aback. 'How…' Her eyes lit with realisation. 'Erika. Oh, Xavier, I'm so sorry.'

'Don't be,' he said gruffly. 'It's been over three years. Long done.'

'It might have happened a while ago, but those emotions—regret, disappointment, hurt—tend to linger.' She fell silent and he watched her face with a frown, wondering what she was talking about. But she cleared her throat and continued before he could spend any more time thinking about it. 'But yes, you're right. The doctor seems to think the time is right for us to try IUI by the end of this week. We'd have to monitor it to find the best day, but…if we want to do this, it'll be the right time.'

He held his breath, ignoring the food that was going cold in front of him, and then released it unsteadily. 'This is all happening so fast.'

'I know. But there's no guarantee it'll work.'

He nodded, knowing the truth of that all too well. 'And if it does work?'

'Then we have our protection against Zacchaeus. We announce our wedding after the insemination, and we can tell our people it was a honeymoon baby when she or he comes. Which would mean we would have to push to have the wedding in two months at the most.'

'I didn't mean about that,' Xavier said softly. 'I want to know what happens with *us* if this works.'

'We'll be married and become parents,' she replied stiffly. 'We'll rule our kingdoms together. We'll protect them. That's all.'

'And you think it'll be that simple?'

'It has to be,' she said through clenched teeth now.

'Just because it has to be doesn't mean it will be.'

'Stop pushing, Xavier.'

'Or what?' he asked, doing exactly what she'd told him not to. He shifted the plate in front of him and leaned forward. 'What will happen if I keep pushing?'

Her eyes flashed. 'You might not like what you find.'

CHAPTER FIVE

'I THINK I *will* keep pushing,' Xavier replied. 'I might finally find the answers to questions I've had for years.'

Fired up, she sat back. 'Fine. Let's get it out of the way so you can get over it. Ask me what it is you want to know.'

'Why did you really break up with me?'

'Because I realised how much the crown would require of me, and I couldn't have given Aidara what it deserved if we'd been together.'

'What does that mean?'

'You know what it means.' When he shook his head, she clenched her teeth. 'Have you suddenly forgotten all the things our families told us?'

'Refresh my memory.'

'You know what I'm talking about,' she said impatiently. 'You know they had their doubts about our relationship.'

'I remember us deciding that their doubts had no foundation.'

'Yes. Until I actually became Queen and started asking myself whether I *was* using our relationship to run away from my responsibilities. And whether you *were* distracting me.'

'And your answer to that was that you were? And that I was?'

'I… Yes,' she faltered.

She remembered how much she'd wanted him by her side after her coronation. How much she'd rather have spent time with him than deal with her new life. How much she'd longed to go back to that day on the beach with him. Happy. Peaceful. Without the weight of the world on her shoulders.

She'd spent too long dwelling on it when she should have been thinking about her new responsibilities. About how she would be Queen to a grieving nation. How she would grieve herself. For her father and her King. For her mother, and the woman she'd thought her mother had been.

She should have spent her time trying to come to terms with all the duties her life would now revolve around. Duties which hadn't included Xavier.

When she'd realised that he'd become more important to her than her responsibilities as

Queen, she'd panicked. She couldn't have allowed that. She couldn't have allowed her grandmother's predictions about their relationship to become a reality. She couldn't have allowed the fears that some day they *would* distract her, keep her from giving her kingdom her all.

'My people needed my attention. My full attention. And dedication. Me being with you… It didn't allow for that. It wouldn't have.'

'So none of it was because you didn't love me?'

She pushed out of her seat, needing distance between them. But as soon as she did, he followed. 'What does it matter, Xavier? We moved on. *You* moved on. Wasn't it three months after we ended things that you started dating Erika?'

'Was I supposed to wait for you, Leyna?' he snapped. 'You told me you didn't love me, and that you wouldn't marry me. Was I supposed to wait for you after that?'

'You were supposed to mourn me like I mourned *you*,' she shot back, angry tears forming in her eyes. She waited for them to go away—she *would not* cry in front of him—and then said, 'I didn't expect you to wait, but the least you could have done was give it more than three months.'

'You mourned?' he asked softly then.

'Of course I mourned. I'd lost my best friend.'

'But not the man you loved?'

'Oh, for heaven's sake.' She turned to him. 'I loved you, Xavier. I only told you I didn't because I knew you wouldn't let me go otherwise.' Her eyes started to fill again, and she allowed herself a moment of weakness when she said, 'You were an idiot who insulted everything we had for believing I didn't.'

He moved quickly—so quickly that her mind hadn't had the chance to process it before his lips were on hers. The rational part of her mind told her that she should stop him— that she would regret it if she didn't. But in that moment she allowed herself to be carried away by finally—*finally*—kissing him again.

His lips were soft. They moved gently against hers, as though kissing her was completely normal. As though it was something he was used to doing. Warmth went through her body, settling low in her belly. It demanded she move closer, so she did. Her hands settled on his waist, and when she felt the slight tremble beneath them she pressed even closer, sliding her arms around his body.

Her body shivered as it felt the muscle, the strength, the *maleness* of him.

And then she felt her body dissolve when his hands ran over it, sending frissons she had no control over juddering through her. She gave a small moan when his tongue touched hers. Groaned when it moved inside her mouth. Every nerve in her body felt raw, every bone as though it were melting. She couldn't remember wanting—*needing*—anything more than she did Xavier right in that moment.

The whirring of a helicopter flying above them brought her back to reality. She'd forgotten about the pictures, she realised, and moved to step away from him. But he put a hand on her back, his eyes telling her that she couldn't leave their embrace without ruining the photo op.

So Leyna stood there, her body still touching his, her lips still pulsing from their kiss. The fire that had consumed her only a few seconds earlier turned to ice as she realised what they'd just done. As she realised what it would mean for her now that she knew what it was like to kiss him again. Now that she could no longer ignore the emotions she'd shunned for the last decade.

Worse still, she could feel him pull away from her. It was confirmed when the helicopter finally flew off and he let go of her and strode back to their table.

'I suppose this isn't needed any more,' he said in a tone that told her he had no intention of talking about what had just happened.

Too bad.

'Why did you kiss me?'

'I saw the helicopter. Thought it would make a great picture.'

She stared at him, wondering if it was true. And thought that if it was there'd be another crack added to her already broken heart.

'We can discuss the rest of this now, or we can choose to do so later,' she said, making sure her voice gave away none of her hurt.

'Now. But let's make it quick.'

She nearly laughed. But then she took a moment to process, and walked back to the table and sat down. She picked up her knife and fork and started eating the meal that had gone cold, not tasting a thing. She heard his chair scrape against the floor when he followed her lead, and they ate the food in utter silence.

She knew it was stubbornness—from both of them—but they didn't speak until the food had been cleared. Then she sat back and said, 'Rules for this marriage. There can't be anyone else.'

'Why would there be?'

'I don't know, Xavier,' she said dryly. 'Why *would* there be?'

She saw that he'd got her implication when his eyes flashed. 'If there's any kind of *commitment* between us—marriage or a child—you have my word that there won't be anyone else for me. How about you?'

Now she did laugh. 'There won't be anyone else.'

'You sound sure.'

'I am sure. Not only because of the common sense of it, but because I'm not interested in there being anyone else.' She immediately realised it sounded as though she was talking about there not being anyone besides *him*, and quickly added, 'I'd rather focus on my duty. As you well know.'

'You won't regret that?' he asked, ignoring her slip. 'You've never been married. You haven't even dated, really.'

'Keeping tabs?'

'It's not keeping tabs when your life is national news.'

She tilted her head but didn't press. 'I won't regret it. I haven't, these past years.'

'Why haven't you?'

Her eyes didn't leave his. 'I already told you.'

'Fine, then tell me this. Does you not dating mean you haven't...*been* with anyone?'

'How is that any of your business?' she snapped, her heart racing. It wasn't something she was ashamed of—and she sure as hell didn't think that it defined her. But she didn't want *him* to know that she was still a virgin. That the closest she'd come to making love to anyone had been with him, on the day he'd proposed. That the memory had been so treasured that she hadn't wanted to spoil it by sleeping with anyone else.

That in the deepest, stupidest part of her heart she was still holding out for him...

'It's not,' he answered, but the glint in his eye told her he'd got the answer he wanted.

It had her grinding her teeth, but she told herself to return to the purpose of their discussion. The sooner they did, the sooner they would finish and the sooner she'd be able to deal with the emotions whirling inside her stomach, making her feel ill.

'There has to be a big engagement,' she heard herself say. 'And a ball after, celebrating.'

'I don't think that's necessary.'

'That would happen if we were marrying under normal circumstances, Xavier. You were the one who wanted us to make this believable,' she reminded him when he lifted his eyebrows.

'And this would be our engagement announcement, I assume?'

'Yes.'

'You already have something in mind, don't you?'

She felt her cheeks heat, but she straightened her spine. 'The Aidaraen Tropical Fruit Festival is next week. I thought announcing our engagement in the orchard would work nicely.'

'And there will already be a ball to celebrate the winner, so it won't require too much extra effort. Which will save time,' he added, and then nodded. 'I'm fine with that.'

'Good.' There was more, she knew. But there were too many details to anticipate, so she told herself that they would have to discuss them as they came up. Which brought them to the baby. Her heart thudded, and that sick feeling in her stomach grew more urgent.

'The baby,' she started, but stopped when she saw the shake of his head.

'Let's simplify this part. You can let me know when I'm needed for the IUI.'

'You're happy with that? The IUI, I mean. With it happening so quickly, too.'

'I'm not happy about any of this, Leyna. But, as you said, duty comes first.' He stood. 'I'll see you for the procedure.'

He didn't give her a chance to respond before walking away, and it took her a few minutes before she'd fully realised he was gone. She pushed out of her chair and went to the edge of the rooftop, standing in one of the grooves that allowed her to see the Aidaraen orchard at the top of a green hill and the beaches just beyond it.

She should do this more often, she thought. She should come and take a look at the beautiful land, at the people carrying out their daily tasks. At the place she had to take care of and the people she had to protect. It reminded her that the pain throbbing with each beat of her heart was worth it. That working with the man she'd once loved—that marrying him—despite how much it threw her off balance, was worth it.

And that living the life she'd always dreamed of despite circumstances from hell was worth it.

It *was* worth it, she thought again, but it was threatening to break her, not just throw her off balance. She could almost feel the progress she'd made in the past ten years being eroded. Again, her responsibility to her kingdom was requiring her to forget about Leyna the woman. To sacrifice *everything* that woman had done to protect herself from unimaginable hurt and focus on what Leyna the Queen had to do.

Which, up until the State Banquet, she'd been fine with.

Though not *entirely*, she thought, as she remembered all the times her stomach would jump at seeing Xavier over the last ten years, every time they'd had a political meeting. Or the hope her heart would beat with in that very first moment, before she'd remembered the reality of her decision meant that there *was* no hope.

It would be worse now. Now, she would have the reminder of that decision every time she looked at Xavier, her *husband*. Every time she looked at *their child*.

Her heart felt as though it had caught fire. She turned, leaning her back against the wall and closing her eyes in a desperate attempt to control the pain. *This* was why she should have thought more about this plan. *This* was why she should have given herself the chance to grieve—again—for the life she'd wanted but would never have before going through with this plan.

The prospect of having that life without the love she'd thought would accompany it was heartbreaking. And in the next week that prospect would become reality, and that reality would include the *pretence* of love. It would include kisses that made her want and need as a woman, and threaten every part of her that was Queen.

She gave herself a moment to dread it, and then fortified the shield around her heart. She *would* survive this. And surviving meant that she needed to put her personal feelings aside and focus on her duty.

Again.

Leyna glanced back at the kingdom she was serving, felt it remind her of her purpose. She squared her shoulders. She'd served with a broken heart before, so she knew that she could do it again. Satisfied, she strode back to her library.

She had a kingdom to run.

CHAPTER SIX

IT HAD BEEN a mistake.

Safely back on Mattan, it was all Xavier could think about—that kissing Leyna had been a mistake. It had also been an involuntary reaction to hearing that she'd loved him. That she hadn't broken up with him because she hadn't loved him, and that she'd wanted him to wait for her.

It was night now, the sea breeze cooling his heated body where he stood on the balcony of his bedroom. It helped him breathe, that familiar smell of salt and water. And breathing had become difficult the moment he'd touched his lips to Leyna's and had experienced the feel— the taste—of her mouth again.

It had been better than the memories. Better than the dreams he'd had about it even though he'd fought so hard to suppress them. But now that he'd done it, he didn't know how to deal with the emotions it had awoken in him. How *could* he deal with the hurt, the anger, the guilt that kiss had awoken?

He felt the hurt of the words with which she'd ended things between them as sharply as the day she'd said them. And he felt the anger that she'd lied to him about her feelings then. Now that anger was compounded by the fact that she actually *had* loved him. As was the hurt that she'd told him the thing that would hurt him most to make him leave.

And then there was the guilt. *He'd* kissed *her* before he'd even seen that damn helicopter. He thanked the heavens for it now, that he could blame that for his moment of insanity. Because if he'd been in his sane mind he would have never kissed Leyna. No, he wanted to keep things between him and Leyna as professional as possible.

For Erika.

The reminder—and the wave of guilt that came with it—had him gripping the railing of his balcony. He should be thinking of his wife, and all he owed her. He shouldn't be thinking about what would have happened if he hadn't succumbed to his family's urges that he marry. If he hadn't been reminded of *his* duty. If he'd just waited a few more months for Leyna…

The thought was a punch in the gut and he slammed a hand down against the railing, ignoring—no, *welcoming*—the pain that came with it. Erika had sacrificed her dreams to be married to him. And they had been happy in the beginning.

But that was because she'd actually tried in the beginning.

He hated the thought, but he couldn't deny its truth. Erika had been an exemplary queen at first. She'd joined him on all his duties, and had done so with poise and dignity. Even when it was clear that his people didn't quite like the idea of her as much as they had Leyna. Even when the media turned against her.

They'd been relentless in their judgement, in their comparisons to Leyna. They'd called Erika the consolation prize, had printed headlines screaming that she would always be second place in their King's heart.

It had been tough—on both of them. Especially as Xavier had still been trying to convince himself that being in a relationship with Erika—that marrying her—was best for his kingdom. He'd tried to push it away when Erika had asked him about it. When she'd accused him of exactly what those headlines had said.

He'd told her not to worry, that he was committed to her and only her. And he'd done his utmost to convince her—and maybe even himself—of that. But then Erika had started to recoil from doing public events. He'd had to cajole, convince and eventually beg her to join him. And when she had, she'd done so from behind a shield even he couldn't penetrate.

Then there'd been their struggle to have a child, which would have tested any marriage. In a royal marriage it had been amplified. More so when that marriage had already been on shaky ground.

If he'd had the chance to do it all over again, he would have done it so differently. He would have worked harder to make sure Erika knew he was committed to *her*. That, despite the way they'd come together and the troubles they'd inevitably faced during their relationship, he loved her no matter what.

Those were the what-ifs he needed to think about. Not the ones with Leyna. If he was going to dwell on the past, it should be on his relationship with Erika and how he could do better for her now.

He didn't have to think too hard about that. He knew how he could do it. He had to stop fantasising about a life with Leyna that he would never have. It didn't matter that they were going through the formality of marriage and a child—their responsibility to their kingdoms was the reason for that. There was no emotion behind the decision, and absolutely no cause for him to ever have to kiss her again. Unless it was for show.

He could do that. He *would* do that. For Erika.

'Your Majesty…the Queen is on the telephone for you.'

Of course she is, Leyna thought, and waved a hand to indicate that she would take her grandmother's call. Her grandmother *would* call the morning the doctor had given Leyna the go-ahead for the insemination. Xavier was on his way, which had already knotted her stomach, and now she had to deal with her grandmother.

She sighed and picked up the phone.

'Hello, Granny.' Leyna forced cheer into her voice. 'It's lovely to hear from you. Are you enjoying South Africa?'

'I haven't called to exchange pleasantries, Leyna.' Kathleen's sharp voice would have made Leyna wince if she hadn't expected it. 'I've heard about Kirtida. I should have heard about it from you. A month ago.'

'You would have known about it if you'd returned for the State Banquet as I requested.'

'So you've kept me uninformed about what's happening in my home as punishment?'

'Of course not.' *But didn't you leave your home?* 'I just didn't want to worry you when we didn't have any cause for concern.'

'There was cause for concern the moment Zacchaeus overthrew his father. Surely you know that?'

'Yes, I do. Which is why Xavier and I have done everything we possibly can to get in touch with Zacchaeus to talk it all through.'

'Have you succeeded?'

Leyna closed her eyes. 'Unfortunately not. But it's allowed us insight into where we stand, and we have a plan.'

'I'm listening.'

She'll find out soon enough anyway. 'Xavier and I will be getting married.'

A stony silence followed her words, and then her grandmother spoke again. 'Are you marrying the King of Mattan, or the man you're still in love with?'

'I'm not—' She broke off, sucked in a breath. 'Does it matter?'

'Yes, it does.' Kathleen's voice had softened, and it was so unexpected that her next words sliced through the shield Leyna always wore with her grandmother. 'Love is a wonderful thing, but when you lose it you lose sight of what's important. Just look at your mother.'

Her words pierced the wound Leyna had always tried to protect.

'Your duty is most important.'

'Yes, Granny,' Leyna said in a hoarse voice. 'I know.'

'So are you marrying for duty or for love?'

'For duty. To protect Aidara.'

There was relief in her grandmother's voice when she replied. 'Good.'

'I must say goodbye now. I have an urgent appointment. Keep well, Granny.'

She put down the phone before her grandmother could reply, and stood.

And then sat back down when her legs started to shake.

She clenched her fists when she saw that her hands were shaking, too, and told herself to breathe when the familiar throb of pressure grew in her chest. And while she fought to keep herself from having a panic attack, she reminded herself that her grandmother's advice was based on her own experiences.

Just as she had when her grandmother had handed out her warnings about Xavier.

Leyna knew how much Kathleen had hurt after her husband had died. And then she'd lost her son, too, and her purpose in life along with him. She hadn't seen supporting Leyna as a purpose. And when she'd grieved for her son, she'd channelled her energy into the sense of purpose that had been kindled after her husband's death. The crown. And when Leyna's father had died, the only remaining link to Kathleen's husband and child.

But it was only the crown that she cared about, and not the granddaughter who wore it. Duty had become an obsession, and Leyna was subject to her grandmother's opinions on her ruling, marrying and bearing an heir. It had made a tough job even tougher, and Leyna had to keep reminding herself of why Kathleen was like that.

She reminded herself of it on the days when she felt alone, when her grandmother's sharp tongue spoke of responsibility and not family. It made her miss her mother even more, as Helene had never allowed her mother-in-law to dictate to Leyna as she had to Leyna's father.

But thinking about her mother would send her into a panic, and Leyna had erected a shield to protect her from distressing interactions with her grandmother. It was just that on days like today, when Leyna already felt vulnerable, she let her shield down.

She didn't have any more time to give in to it when Carlos knocked on her door. She laid a hand on her chest—still tight, but she was past the possibility of an attack now—and then she straightened her shoulders and followed him to the room that had been prepared for the insemination.

Xavier was already there, his face set in a grim expression that had her stomach tumbling.

'Is everything okay?'

'Yes.'

'No, it's not.'

'Of course it's not,' he hissed and strode to the door, shutting it with a bang. 'This is a terrible idea.'

She kept her voice calm. 'Have you changed your mind?'

'No,' he snapped, running a hand over his forehead. 'I just… I don't think this…' He blew out a breath. 'What if this doesn't work?'

'Then we try again next month.'

'And what if *that* doesn't work?'

'We try IVF.'

'That might not work either.'

'There's no reason it shouldn't.' But his words had their intended effect, and she swallowed the bile that rose to her throat.

'Leyna,' he said, his voice sounding like a plea. 'I told you how long Erika and I tried. We tried IUI. We failed.'

'We won't fail,' she insisted.

'How are you so calm about this?'

'Because I have to be. This is our future. The future of our kingdoms.'

But she wasn't calm. In fact, Leyna could only remember feeling *less* calm ten years ago. Right before she'd told Xavier she didn't love him. The panic in her chest was back in full force now and made its way higher, clutching at her throat. She went over to the side of the bed where a jug of water stood, and drank as though her life depended on it.

She closed her eyes and when she had control of herself again turned back to Xavier. He still had a troubled expression on his face, and perhaps that was the reason he just nodded and said, 'Let's get it over with then.'

She watched him open the door and call for the doctor. And then, before she knew it, she was on the bed with her legs open, watching the doctor prepare the catheter that would place Xavier's sperm into her uterus.

'Stop!' she said when he settled at her feet, no longer able to ignore the panic.

'What's wrong?' Xavier asked at her side.

'You were right,' she said as her chest started to heave. 'This is a terrible idea.'

'Are *you* changing your mind now?'

'Yes, I am.'

'Your Majesty?' her doctor queried.

'Give us a moment, please,' Xavier instructed.

When they were alone he turned back to her. 'What's going on, Leyna?'

'I told you. I don't want to do this.' She put a hand on her chest, hoping it would somehow help her to breathe easier.

'I thought you were fine with all this. For our kingdoms.'

'I *had* to say that. You were panicking.' She squeezed her eyes shut. 'But everything you said makes sense. This might not work. And if it doesn't, what do we have to protect our kingdoms?'

'Our marriage.' His voice was sure, the earlier hesitation in his tone gone.

'And what if...what if something happens to me?'

He took her hand. 'Is that what you're scared of?'

'My kingdom needs me.' She turned her head to him now, the fears she didn't want to reveal spilling out of her mouth. 'If something happens to me, who will look out for my people? And what if I can't be a mother? What if I can't do *this*? What if I can't be a wife?'

'Breathe,' he said sharply, but his grip on her hand squeezed reassuringly, softening his words. Helplessly she obeyed, and forced air into her lungs. And then did it again and again, until she felt calmer. Or at least until embarrassment set in.

She swallowed. 'I'm sorry—'

'Don't apologise.' He shook his head. 'This is an…extreme situation. Neither of us could have anticipated the way we've reacted.' Though she appreciated the words she didn't reply, and he continued quietly. 'Nothing's going to happen to you. And if it does—' he cleared his throat '—I'll make sure Aidara is taken care of. As for the rest of it… Leyna, you're the strongest woman I know. And the bravest. You can do this. You can be a mother, and a wife, *and* a queen. And you can get through this procedure.'

She bit her lip. 'Thank you.'

'It's true. You can do this.' He paused. 'Unless you don't want to because you no longer believe it's the best thing for our kingdoms.'

It was a reminder of why they were doing it. And when she looked at his face she saw that he'd meant it to be. She pulled herself together and then nodded.

'Call the doctor.'

'Are you sure?'

'No,' she said, but gave him a small smile. 'Call him.'

He did, and the doctor came back. His face was clear of expression, though he hesitated when he sat down at her feet again. She nodded at him, but turned away from the screen he was using when he began to guide the catheter into her uterus.

She closed her eyes and bit her lip, praying that she wouldn't start crying. She felt a warm, strong hand grip hers, and then she heard Xavier's voice in her ear.

'It's going to be fine, Leyna. Whatever happens, we'll handle it together.'

She bit down on her lip even harder, her only response tightening her hold on his hand. She held her breath and a few minutes later the procedure was done.

'As I explained earlier, I'd like you to rest for a while,' Leyna's doctor told her. 'I'd even advise that you take it easy for the rest of the day, too. After that, you can go ahead as normal.'

'Thank you, Doctor,' she murmured, and pulled the covers over her. When the doctor left, she cleared her throat.

'I'm sorry about all of that.'

'I told you, you don't have to apologise.'

She nodded and then said, 'You don't have to stay. You've done your part.'

'I'd like to,' he said very quietly. 'If you don't mind.'

She shook her head in answer, and just closed her eyes. They sat like that for a while, and Leyna used the time to make sure that her emotions were in check. It was the enormity of the procedure that had made her feel so emotional, so uncertain, she told herself. Though she knew there was more to it than that, she forced herself not to dwell on it.

But the longer the silence stretched, the more she found herself wanting to know what that *more* was. And, since it sat heavy in her throat, she worried she might not be able to control herself if she thought about it any more. So she sighed in relief when Xavier finally spoke.

'Are you okay?'

'Fine.'

'Leyna.'

The tone of his voice had her opening her eyes, and she turned to look at him. Her heart ached at the expression on his face. It was kind and compassionate, and looked so much like *her* Xavier that she wanted to sob.

'This was a huge step today,' Leyna forced herself to say in a calm voice. 'I just need some…time.'

'Of course,' he replied. 'But I just want you to know that if you want to talk…well, I'm a good listener.'

She squeezed her eyes shut again, but it was no use. She felt the tears trailing down her cheeks, and was horrified when he brushed them away. More so when she felt the bed dip and his arms go around her.

Her eyes flew open. 'What…what are you doing?'

'I'm holding you.'

'You don't—'

'I know I don't have to,' he replied mildly, and then drew her in tighter to him. It didn't send that spark of electricity through her as touching him normally did, though there was a slight buzz of heat that reminded her of her attraction to him.

But no, this was purely comfort and, before she could help herself, she snuggled closer.

There were no more tears, she realised, and told herself to inform him he didn't have to hold her any more. But her heart asked for a few more moments—just long enough for it to memorise being in Xavier's arms again. As she gave in to it, she felt herself drifting off.

In the arms of the man she'd once loved.

CHAPTER SEVEN

XAVIER WASN'T SURE whether he could explain the emotion that had him climbing onto that bed. He'd felt fear and panic just before the procedure, and had almost given in to it. Now that he had time to think about it, he knew that was partly because he and Erika had gone through the same thing so many times with the prospect of failure looming over them, almost punishingly.

With him and Leyna now, the stakes were even higher. And the prospect of failure more menacing. When Leyna had told him to snap out of it, he'd been annoyed. Angry. And then she'd broken down, and he'd realised her reaction revealed her own fear.

Perhaps that was why he'd got onto that bed. The fact that the unfeeling Queen of Aidara wasn't so unfeeling after all. Or perhaps it had been everything that she'd said. And the emotion that had hit him in the gut when she'd said it.

He knew she was right. Especially as she'd voiced his own fears. The IUI was a desperate attempt to save their kingdoms, and if it didn't work… He took a shaky breath, his arms tightening around Leyna. He didn't want to let her down as he had Erika. No, he corrected himself. He didn't want to let his *kingdom* down in the same way he had before. With Erika.

But he also knew that what she'd said before the panic had gripped her had been right. If this round didn't work, they would do another. And then they would try IVF. And they would keep trying.

He ignored the pain in his chest at the prospect of going through the struggle of infertility again. And told himself the pain wasn't worse now because he was putting Leyna through it, too. No, time had just faded the memory of the pain, and now that he was feeling it again, made it *seem* worse than it had been before. He had to convince himself extra hard of that since he was lying on Leyna's bed, holding her. Since he hadn't felt more complete in years. He closed his eyes, memorising the sweet floral smell of her and the way she fitted into his arms so perfectly. As he rested his head on hers, he smiled, thinking her curls provided enough support and softness that it could be a pillow.

It was the last thought he had before he heard her gasp.

He sat up just as she did, and then shifted off the bed when she put her arms out, indicating that she wanted space. Helpless, he watched as she set a shaky hand on her heaving chest, and felt his heart twist as she calmed herself. When she did, she looked at him, her eyes a little wild, though embarrassment obscured it.

'I'm sorry,' she said with a forced smile. 'Bad dream.'

He nodded and returned to the chair where he'd sat during the procedure. 'About what?'

'I don't remember.'

'You're lying.'

'I'm not,' she denied. 'But I *am* hungry. I think I'll call down for something. Would you like anything?'

'No.' He waited for her to call the kitchen and then asked, 'How often do you have these dreams?'

'On and off.'

'About the same thing?'

'I told you—I don't remember what it was about,' she said, and he saw a muscle jump in her brow. Knowing that she needed to avoid stress, he didn't push.

'How are you feeling?'

'Fine.'

'Really?'

'Yes, really. You can leave now, if you want.'

'Do *you* want me to leave?'

Her eyes told him that she didn't, and he felt warmth creep into his heart. But she only said, 'It's completely up to you, Xavier.'

'Then I think I'll stay.'

He wasn't sure why he wanted to, especially after his resolution the night before. Especially after what had transpired that afternoon. But the arrival of her food distracted him from pondering it. His mouth watered, reminding him that he hadn't eaten since that morning.

'Would you like me to call down for something for you, too?' Leyna asked, her eyes lit with dull amusement. 'Before you drool all over my food?'

'No, thank you. I'm fine.'

'When was the last time you ate anything?'

'This morning. But I'm not hungry.'

A tight ache in his stomach cursed him for lying, and a moment later Leyna leaned over to the phone beside the bed and called the kitchen for something to be sent up for him as well.

'You didn't have to do that.'

'I know, but you were lying. And being the proud man that you are, you wouldn't have said anything even though your eyes have already eaten my meal in the minutes we've been discussing this.'

He refused the smile that threatened. 'Thank you.'

She nodded, and then intertwined her fingers.

He frowned. 'You should start eating. Before your soup gets cold.'

'It's a bit too hot at the moment, so it needs to get cold.'

'You're waiting for me, though, aren't you?'

When she lifted her shoulders—exactly *how* did she manage to make the action look graceful?—he shook his head.

'You're a stubborn woman, Leyna.'

'We always used to have that in common,' she replied.

Silence followed her words, and he wondered if this was how their future together was going to be. Stilted small talk, never about anything personal, only dealing with necessities. But sometimes—like when she'd panicked about the procedure, like when she'd been so emotional it had led her to tears—things were *so* personal between them that both of them had to ignore it.

It complicated matters that she might be carrying his child. His heart beat so hard in his chest at that thought—one he hadn't allowed himself right until that moment. Why did the prospect make him so happy? Was it because this was Leyna? Or was it because he was getting another chance at having the child he'd always wanted?

Both options made him feel ill, because it felt like betraying Erika. But he'd always known he must have a child. He had to have an heir. There was no other option. But he'd wanted a child with his wife. And he felt as if he'd failed her because that hadn't happened for them.

He *still* felt as if he'd failed her, because now it was a possibility for him and Leyna.

He told himself that it was for the good of his kingdom. And reminded himself that with marriage and a baby on the way, his mother and grandmother would finally stop nagging him to marry again. He'd listened to them the first time and, because his father had added weight to it, he'd married Erika.

But the heartbreak following her death had given him a reason to resist the next relationship his mother and grandmother had attempted to push him into. And now, with marriage and a possible child in his future, he would finally be free of the pressure from his family—to produce an heir for the sake of the crown. To prevent him from falling short of the legacy of the men in his family.

He hadn't thought about any of it until that moment, sitting across from Leyna, waiting for his food to arrive.

A sigh of relief released from his lungs when it did, and he busied himself with the meal, ignoring the look Leyna had given him at the sound. They ate in silence but it was woefully short and, before he knew it, Leyna was arranging for their food to be taken away.

'Thank you,' she said when they were alone.

'For what?'

'For allowing this to happen on Aidara.'

'Were you afraid I would insist that this intensely personal procedure be done on Mattan?'

'Maybe,' she said with a small smile. 'Perhaps irrationally. In my fear about all of this.' She paused. 'It helped, to have it done here in my home.' When she looked at him there was something so vulnerable in her expression that it had the feelings he'd tried to banish the night before stirring again. 'After dealing with something like this... It's nice to be somewhere familiar.'

'Of course,' he said softly. 'Is that what you felt earlier? Fear?'

'The dream?' He shook his head. 'Oh, you mean the panic. And the tears.' She looked down at her hands. 'I suppose so. Yes.' Seconds passed in silence but he didn't reply, knowing she wasn't done. 'This is scary.'

'I know it is.'

'Are you scared?'

He wanted to take her hand again but he only said, 'You know I am.'

'So you feel like a coward, too?' Now he heard the anguish in her voice. 'Like we shouldn't be questioning this because it's something we're doing for our people. To protect them.'

He took a moment before he replied. 'We're still human, Leyna. We both have fears, and anxieties. Especially about this.' He fell silent when he thought about his own fears, his own anxieties, but then pushed on. 'But we can't let them keep us from doing what we need to do for our people. To protect them.'

She nodded, and there was a long pause before she spoke again. 'Do you know how long it's been since I last cried? Years,' she said, answering his silent head-shake.

'What did you cry about?'

'My life falling apart.' She bit her lip as though she'd said too much, and then she turned her head to face him. 'It was after I found out my mother had left, after…after I'd ended things with you.' She looked away at that. 'I'd lost everyone I cared about. All I had left was an uninterested grandmother and responsibility for the lives of millions of people.'

'So you told yourself you couldn't waste time grieving and focused instead on running your kingdom.'

'Exactly.' Her lips curved. 'We're still so alike, aren't we?'

'More than either of us want, I'm guessing.'

She laughed. 'You wouldn't be wrong.'

There was silence again and then she asked, 'Is that how you felt after Erika died?'

He felt something tighten inside him, but he answered, 'Yes.'

'And you feel guilty about it.'

It wasn't a question, and it made him snap his next words. 'Do you?'

She didn't seem upset by his reaction, only shaking her head. 'I *did* grieve for my father. But I was allowed to. Expected to. But the others… Well, one of them was because I'd chosen it, and so I kept those feelings to myself and never let them influence the way I ran the kingdom. The other…' She trailed off and took a breath. 'My mother left me with only a note saying goodbye. I didn't think she deserved me mourning her.'

Again, he found himself wanting to reach out and take her hand. To comfort her, to ask how she'd coped with the loss of both her parents so close together. There was a part of him that felt as though he should have been there for her. That accused him of abandoning her when she'd needed him the most.

But a bigger part reminded him that he *couldn't* have been there for her. It would have killed him to go back to being just friends with her. It didn't ease the guilt or the regret, though it did make him wonder, again, whether things would have been different if he'd just given it some time. If he'd just ignored his father's reminder of the need to do his duty.

'Erika's death was so unexpected,' he said suddenly. It took him a moment to realise he'd said it to remind himself of the pact he'd made the night before. 'I woke up early that morning to do something—I can't even remember what it was now—and when I got back to the room she was gone.'

She reached for his hand immediately, squeezing. 'I'm so sorry, Xavier.'

He nodded. 'It was some time after her funeral that I realised I couldn't go on in that state. So I told myself that living would be my way of celebrating her, and her life.'

'It's an honourable way of looking at it,' she said quietly, her hand lifting from his. 'Beautiful, too. Though I'm not surprised. You both always had so much light together.'

His heart stalled. 'You thought that?'

'Yes. I thought it the moment I saw you look at each other on your wedding day.'

His world swirled, and then straightened almost abruptly.

'You weren't at the wedding. You were meeting with the South African president about the trade deals between their country and the Isles.'

'I came back. Just to see the ceremony.' She paused. 'You didn't think I would miss my best friend's wedding, did you?'

There was a teasing glint in her eyes, but he saw a lot more there.

Regret. Longing.

A ball of tension began bouncing in his chest.

'We weren't best friends then, though. We weren't anything.'

'Maybe,' she allowed. 'But I still cared about you. You can't just switch off twenty years of caring,' she added, as though he didn't know that himself. 'I wanted to share one of the most important days in your life, even if it was just in the form of an obscured view from the crowd. But because I wasn't supposed to be there, I made sure no one saw me. Of course, Jacob helped with that.'

Xavier sifted through his memories of that day, trying to recall whether he'd seen her bodyguard there. He knew he hadn't seen her. He'd never forgotten the relief he'd felt because of it. But it wasn't a surprise that he didn't remember seeing Jacob. He'd taken care to ensure his eyes were only on his bride that day. He hadn't wanted to give any grounds to the speculation in the media. He was marrying Erika because he wanted to. Not because he couldn't have Leyna.

But that wasn't quite true, was it?

He closed his eyes.

'I've upset you. I'm sorry, I didn't mean to.'

'You haven't upset me.' He opened his eyes again, his heart trembling at the angst he saw in hers. 'I suppose it was just that I didn't think you cared enough to attend.'

'I know that's my fault. And I completely accept that it is. But I told you I mistook my love for you as a friend for romantic love.' She lifted a shoulder. 'Even in that I was still telling you I loved you.'

He didn't have an answer to that. To him, her words had meant she'd felt nothing for him. Her actions had supported that, too. Was he now supposed to believe she'd loved him as a friend all along, even when she'd treated him so poorly? Caring about someone meant caring about their feelings, too. It had been clear to him then that she hadn't cared about his feelings, or else she'd never have done what she did.

'So, we'll try again if we don't fall pregnant this time,' he said, focusing instead on the future. On parts of the future that he *could* control.

'Yes,' she replied. 'But there's no reason for us not to.' She held up a hand when he opened his mouth to protest. 'I know what I said earlier. As I told you, I was scared. I still am. But we *have* to focus on the positives if we want to get through this. And the positive here is that there's no medical reason for us not to fall pregnant. We have to trust in that. If not... Well, like you said, we'll deal with it then.'

He wasn't as prepared for this response as he'd been for her first one. Not when suddenly he was thinking about how differently Erika had approached things. Even *after* she'd had the chance to process.

It made his next words come out more harshly than he'd intended. 'And if we never fall pregnant? What then?'

He watched her struggle for words, and then she said, 'We'll adopt. One child from your kingdom, one from mine. We'll be open about our struggle. We'll be human. And our children will fill the same role.'

'That's unprecedented.'

'And not something we have to think about yet,' she told him. 'But we have options.'

He watched her. Wondered at her. 'Are children really that important to you?'

'Yes,' she said simply. 'I need to make sure Aidara is taken care of. You have your sisters, Xavier, and a nephew to take over from you should anything happen. You'll have even more assurances once Nalini marries. I, on the other hand, only have distant cousins who live in the luxury of being royal but would never survive serving their kingdom. Not the way it deserves. So, I have to make sure that my people are taken care of. The only way I can do that is if I raise their future ruler myself.' She took a breath. 'If it means changing the law—if it means breaking tradition—I will.'

Respect—fierce and solid—erupted in him. 'Your people are lucky to have you, Leyna.'

Her face changed into a charming expression of surprise, and her cheeks coloured slightly. 'As are yours. For a king, I mean.'

He smiled but shook his head. 'I don't think we're on the same level.' Before he could stop himself, his deepest fear spilled out. 'Sometimes I think they deserve more.'

'Why?'

And now that he'd started, he couldn't seem to stop. 'Because they've had more. The kings before me…they were *better*. They didn't make mistakes.'

'What mistakes have you made?'

He let out a short bark of laughter 'What mistakes *haven't* I made?'

'Fine then. Tell me why you think they were better.'

'Because…' He frowned, wondering why he couldn't come up with one specific reason for that belief.

'Because that's what you've been told for the whole of your life.' His gaze caught hers and he felt as if she could see right through him.

'No, there are reasons.'

'Because you believe you've made mistakes they wouldn't have made?'

'Yes!' he exclaimed, almost grateful she'd given him a reason.

'But you can't name one mistake you've made.'

'Leyna, all of this is beside the point.'

'What *is* the point, Xavier?' she asked. 'Because I'd really like to know how you could convince yourself that your people deserve more than a king who'd sacrifice his entire personal life to make sure they were protected.'

Again, he couldn't find the words to speak.

'I know exactly how you feel, Xavier,' she said softly, her hand finding his again. This time, he found his own hand turning over and his fingers sliding through hers. 'That uncertainty? It's part of what we are, of *who* we are. And, yes, it's worse because we have families who constantly point out what they believe are our failures. But we can't give in to that, or to that little voice that tells us they're right.'

She offered him a small smile now that went straight to his heart. 'And now we have each other to remind us of that.'

This was why he'd fallen so hard, he realised. He'd spent his entire youth seeking the light she brought into his life, which had been filled with condemnation *but* for her. Her positivity, her strength, her spirit—they were things he'd tried to forget.

But they were exactly the things that had made that task almost impossible.

When he leaned in for the kiss this time, he watched her eyes widen and then spark with pleasure. And then they closed, as did his, and he sank into the kiss.

It was slow and sweet, filled with an emotion he knew they'd never speak of. The warmth of it rippled through him, unsettling the walls and guards behind which he'd hidden his feelings for her. His free hand lifted to cup her cheek, and then lowered over the curve of her breast—pausing briefly there—

and then settled on her waist. He knew that if he'd let himself explore how her body had changed—if he let himself explore the full softness of her breast—the tone of the kiss would change.

And if the tone of the kiss changed, he might not be able to stop himself from making love to her.

The prospect had him edging away, but she moaned in protest and pulled him towards her. He climbed onto the bed, his body mirroring hers, and let himself take more. Desire stirred from where he'd tried to hide it after their first kiss those few days ago, and he heard its demands in the pounding of his blood in his ears.

'Leyna,' he whispered hoarsely, drawing back. 'We can't do this.'

'Why not?'

He couldn't think of a single reason. He sucked in air and then shook his head. 'You didn't want it to happen like this.'

'I also didn't want it to happen when I was thirty. But it is what it is.' She inched closer.

'Can you honestly tell me you won't regret it?' he asked desperately now. 'It happening like this?'

She hesitated briefly and then said, 'It's just sex.'

'It's *not* just sex.' He pushed up from the bed

now, set his feet on the ground. 'It'll never be just sex. Not for us.'

'Maybe not when we were younger. But we might have just made a baby together, for heaven's sake. Why *not* try it like this, too?'

'This is not the way you want it to happen for the first time.'

He stood, unable to be so close to her now. It only succeeded in testing his control. He was desperately trying not to take her up on her offer.

'That's irrelevant, Xavier—'

'No, Leyna, it's not,' he said sharply. 'I know you well enough to believe that you know that, too.'

He got up and strode out of the room before she could reply.

CHAPTER EIGHT

IF THERE WAS anything more embarrassing than offering herself to a man—only to be rejected—Leyna wasn't sure she'd experienced it. It made things only marginally worse that that man was going to become her husband and the father to her child.

Was it any wonder the air was so tense between her and Xavier as they made their way to the Aidaraen Tropical Fruit Festival?

They were silent as the car travelled the short distance from Aidara's castle to the orchard where the festival was being held. Leyna knew the tension was compounded by the fact that they would be announcing their engagement just after announcing the winner.

And they had no idea how their people would respond.

'Do you think they'll believe I'm only here to judge the contest with you?' Xavier asked, breaking the silence.

'It doesn't matter,' she said demurely. 'Because you're *not* only here to judge the contest with me, and they'll find that out soon enough.'

She heard his impatient sigh but ignored it, and turned her head to look out of the window. There were people lining their path to the orchard, waving the Aidaraen flag and smiling brightly at them.

Another reminder of why she was putting herself through this, she thought, and turned back to Xavier.

'But it is believable,' she said, offering him a soft smile for the sake of the pictures. 'We have guest judges every year. You've been one of them.'

'But not since I married Erika.'

She fixed a smile on her face. 'They'll believe it if we make it convincing. So, try to pretend you can stand the sight of me today.'

'Leyna, you know that's—' He cut off and sighed again. 'If we're going for pretence, you should probably wear this.'

Her eyes fluttered down to find a ring in the palm of his hand. An emerald-cut diamond in a band of rose gold sparkled up at her and she quickly rested her hand over it, her heart thumping in her chest.

'Don't just hand that to me like it's a mint,' she hissed. 'People are taking pictures. If one of them saw it, the festival will be overshadowed by the news.'

'I think the festival will be overshadowed regardless, Leyna,' he said dryly, but slipped the ring back into his jacket pocket.

'Where did you get it anyway?'

'I had it made.'

'For our fake engagement?'

'Yes,' he answered, but something flashed in his eyes that made her doubt the truth of his words.

She didn't want to dwell on it. Not when she was still a little raw from what had happened at the insemination a few days ago. She'd already spent too much time thinking about that day. About how she'd let her panic overcome her. About how she'd started crying when it had been the last thing she'd wanted to do. *And* about how she'd woken up from a dream where Xavier had told her their plan had been a mistake and he'd walked out of her life for ever, her heart hammering in fear.

She'd tried not to think about the fact that he'd witnessed that. Or about their conversation after she'd woken up. *Or* that sweet, passionate kiss that had her melting and wanting at the same time. That had her offering something she hadn't wanted for ten years.

No, she couldn't think about why Xavier

was lying to her about that ring. There was too much else to focus on. Or, she thought more accurately, to *avoid* focusing on.

'This is beautiful,' Xavier said when the car slowed as it reached the road leading to the orchard. She followed his gaze and took in the bright, colourful trees that stood tall and impressive, even though they were still some distance away.

The Royal Aidaraen orchard was the most prominent in the kingdom—where most of their exports came from—and being able to plant on its land was an immense honour for any citizen of Aidara.

There were several contests throughout spring and summer leading up to this one, which ranged from the smallest orchard to the Royal Aidaraen orchard. Winners were allowed to plant on a more prominent piece of land the following year. It took years to reach the Best Fruit of the Kingdom contest in the Fruit Festival, and the winner's fruit was automatically included in Aidara's exports for that year.

The event was prestigious, by invitation only, and that meant every prominent member of society would be there. And that they would witness everything she and Xavier did that day.

'It *is* beautiful,' she answered Xavier. 'And you will say the same to every contestant we speak to today. It is an honour for them to have made it this far, and they will be honoured should they win.'

'You say that as though I've never been to the festival—or been a judge—before.'

'As you so kindly reminded me, that was such a long time ago.' She paused and then added, 'I wasn't sure you'd remember.'

'Of course I remember. I remember all of the festivals I attended. Especially the night of one almost seventeen years ago when we ran away to—'

'Oh, yes,' she interrupted him, feeling her cheeks flush. 'I remember that, too.'

'I don't think you do,' he said. There was no indication on his face that he was teasing her, but the tone of his voice—the unexpected warmth in it—told her he was. 'You told me there was something urgent you needed to tell me. I didn't think you would be so devious as to lie to me, so I followed you down to the beach. And then you told me you'd seen a movie—I don't recall what that movie was—but the girl had been thirteen years old when she'd had her first kiss and since you were thirteen, you thought it was time you had yours, too.'

'Please stop,' Leyna almost groaned. If

they weren't visible to the people in her kingdom she would have covered her face with her hands so he wouldn't be able to see how much he was embarrassing her.

'You pulled me under the palm tree because no one would see us there, and closed your eyes, puckered your lips and waited for me to kiss you.'

Going with it now, she let out a croak of laughter. 'But you didn't know what I expected from you, so you poked me in my stomach and had me opening my eyes again.'

'And I told you that I wasn't going to kiss you because kissing was disgusting.' He smiled now. 'I was lying, by the way. I was too old to think that, but too young to acknowledge that I wanted to kiss you.'

'I didn't know that,' she said, smiling back at him.

'It didn't matter. You gave the biggest sigh I had ever heard in my life and told me that one day I would be grateful you'd been the first girl I'd kiss because no one would know how gross it was.'

'You're welcome,' she said cheekily, and got a grin in return. 'And then I told you to stop talking, to close your eyes, and I kissed you.'

'It was a peck, really, so I'm not sure whether we could call it a kiss.'

'It *was* a kiss,' she answered. 'And you liked it, or you wouldn't have convinced me to try it again.'

'And then again a year later, but this time with tongues.'

'*That* one was gross.'

He chuckled. 'Only because neither of us knew what we were doing. The one after that was fine.'

'I suppose it was.' She was silent, lost in the happiness of the past for a moment. 'How did it end up being so good six years after that?'

'Because we were adults then and had realised there was a little more to kissing than just experimentation.'

She bit her lip. Happiness had quickly turned into regret.

'Being an adult is overrated,' she said, and felt her face heat when she turned back to him and saw he was watching her.

'I'm not sure that's true.'

'Because you're no longer thinking logically,' she said automatically, and nearly gave in to the urge to lean over and show him she wasn't thinking rationally either. It was a great relief when her bodyguard opened the door and the slight breeze floated into the car, bringing her back to reality.

They made their way down the short path

to where a beautiful bronze arch covered with vines indicated the official entrance to the orchard. There was no time to talk about anything then. They spent hours greeting contestants and their families, tasting fruits and posing for photos.

Leyna had been tense at first, fully expecting questions about the state of the alliance to be thrown at her and Xavier. But there was none of that. Instead, the atmosphere was festive and easy.

Leyna felt herself relaxing slowly, though she stiffened whenever Xavier would whisper something in her ear or touch the small of her back. It was for show, she reminded herself. And it was working, too, she thought, as she saw sparks of interest on the faces of those they spoke to.

There was no surprise in those expressions of interest, just a simple acceptance. Some gave her a knowing look, as though they'd expected it. Some nodded to her in approval. It should have alarmed her.

It didn't.

In fact, she was quite comfortable with the looks and smiled in return. As if there was a part of her that mirrored those feelings. She'd only remember that it wasn't reality when she looked at Xavier and saw the carefulness in his eyes.

There hadn't been any of that the day of the insemination. When they'd opened up to each other like they had once before. The hours she'd spent trying not to think about it had, of course, led her to do just that. And every time she came to the same conclusion about why he hadn't wanted to spend the night with her.

He was still in love with his wife.

Though the realisation hurt as much as it had when she'd first read the headline about Xavier and Erika ten years ago, it gave her a reason to keep her distance, too. Especially when he touched her, like he did now, taking her hand to lead her to the privacy of the vineyard at the edge of the orchard so they could decide on the winners, and her stomach flip-flopped.

'How are we possibly supposed to decide?' he asked, dropping her hand as soon as they got there. The lack of contact made her feel a little cold.

'We pretend to be discussing this very carefully, seriously, and we choose someone who needs to win.'

'We don't choose honestly?'

'They were all delicious, weren't they?' she asked, and continued when he nodded. 'Was there one that stood out for you?'

'I'm… Actually, I'm not sure.'

'Exactly, so there were no stand-outs regarding taste, which happens occasionally. When it does, we choose the person who this would mean the most to.' She paused. 'This contest is rarely about the fruit. It's about hope and opportunity. So we choose someone who needs that the most.'

'How would you know that?'

'Because I know *them*. The blonde woman we saw first? Her husband just got diagnosed with cancer. They have two little boys. Winning this could mean they'd get the opportunity to supply some of the local businesses with fruit as well. That would help pay for his chemotherapy. And the brown-haired man we saw last has just opened his own organic wholefoods store. His parents don't support him, and they've told him they'd give him a year before they kicked him out. Winning this could mean a successful business for him and perhaps the pride of his parents.'

'How on earth do you know all this?'

'I do some research on them, and invite them over to the castle for a celebratory dinner before the contest.'

'And they haven't picked up yet that the most down-on-their-luck contestant wins?'

'Oh, it's never clear. Not when everyone has such delicious fruits and I have very careful, serious discussions with my co-judges.' She smiled at him, and then sobered when she saw the look on his face. 'What?'

'I'm just…amazed.' He shook his head and then looked out to the vines in front of them. 'You put so much…*thought* into running your kingdom. Into your people.'

'It's part of the job,' she said, uncomfortable with the praise.

'It should be,' he agreed. 'But it isn't always.' He was silent for a moment. 'And you've sacrificed so much for them.'

'No more than you have.'

It was tempting, so very tempting, to tell him that he—*they*—had been a part of what she'd sacrificed. And that some days she regretted it more than anything else in her life. That sometimes, like their situation now, she resented it for turning her life into something she hadn't anticipated and was very sure she didn't want.

'No, *definitely* more than I have.' He looked at her. 'I've spent most of my time as a king trying to live up to my father's name. To my grandfather's legacy. And here you are, creating your own legacy.'

'You're making me sound much better than I actually am,' she told him. 'I've done the things I've had to, Xavier. That doesn't mean I wanted to do them, or that I was okay with doing them.'

'Like what?'

'Like this.' She gestured between them. 'Do you think I enjoy sacrificing my own sanity to protect my kingdom?'

'Are you saying I make you insane?'

'I'm saying that this entire situation is enough to make the world's sanest person insane. Don't tell me you don't feel it, too.'

'No, I do,' he answered quietly. 'But I'm glad for it. For this opportunity to make up for the mistakes I've made, and to create my own legacy.' He paused. 'I hope some day my people will see that I did this for them, and they'll remember me for it.'

'What are these mistakes you're talking about, Xavier? You keep referring to them, but you can't tell me what they are.'

'I don't *want* to tell you what they are,' he corrected, and she felt her eyes widen.

'No, of course not.' It stung, but she wouldn't let him see that. 'So, we decide on the winner now. I'll put the ring on before we go back, and then we announce the winner, offer our congratulations, and then make the special announcement of our engagement.'

'I moved on, Leyna,' he said instead of answering her. 'We both did. We're not the people who confided in each other as teenagers. Not any more.'

'You say that as though I'm not reminded of it every moment I spend with you.' The words came out less angry than she'd thought they would, tinged with a sadness she saw he'd heard, too.

'Why did you do it?' he asked, and she saw the Xavier she'd hurt that day so long ago. 'The real reason, not the lie you told me.'

'It wasn't—' She broke off when she saw his face. Sighed. 'It wasn't entirely a lie.'

'Okay.' His eyes were deadly serious. 'So tell me why you did it.'

'You told me you weren't able to function properly after Erika died.' It pained her to bring it up, but it was the only way to make him understand. 'Well, that's why. I couldn't *not* function, for Aidara's sake.'

'And you couldn't function with me by your side?'

'No, I couldn't,' she said. 'All those things my grandmother told me? The things your parents told you? I realised they were true. Our friendship—and then more than just a friendship—*was* a distraction. I thought about you constantly, and I kept thinking about…about how they were right. About how I was spending more time thinking about you than I was about my kingdom.'

She paused, her heart pounding at what she'd just said. But she couldn't seem to stop.

'I kept waiting for that to be the reason I failed at my duties. And I thought if I kept thinking that, some day I *would* fail and I would blame you.' She took a breath. 'It was better that I broke up with you. That I didn't blame you for any of it. And that way I could stop anticipating that I would lose you, too. And I could finally let go of that debilitating fear.'

CHAPTER NINE

'WE HAVE TO decide a winner soon,' Leyna said immediately after sending his thoughts into disarray with her words. She was no longer looking at him, but he couldn't bring himself to stop looking at her. Not if there was a chance her face would give away any more clues to her thinking.

'Is that true? Are those the real reasons?'

'Xavier, please,' she whispered, the plea piercing straight through his heart. 'I'm trying to...focus on what we need to do.'

'No, you're avoiding a conversation we should have had a long time ago.' Despite the effect her pleading had on him, he couldn't just let it go. Perhaps because of the stirring of anger he felt building in his chest.

'And maybe we would have had that conversation, Xavier, if you hadn't just given up on us so completely.'

'You're blaming *me* for this?'

'Yes, I think I am.' Anger had splashed her cheeks with colour. 'Do you know what that time in my life was like for me?' She didn't wait for an answer. 'From the moment Carlos called me 'Your Majesty' my life started unravelling. I lost my father and then my mother, and I kept expecting you to leave me, too. I kept waiting for the warnings my grandmother had given me to play out. I kept waiting to fail. The fear of it stayed with me in every single thing I did, and I couldn't think, I couldn't *breathe* without it choking me.'

Her chest heaved and he wanted to take a step forward and tell her to take it easy. To calm down. But her words paralysed him.

'I thought I would get ahead of it and break it off with you. I wanted to be free of that sickening anticipation. I told you I didn't love you but, damn it, I never expected you to believe it.'

'But you knew it was exactly the thing to say to get me to.'

'Maybe. Or maybe I was waiting for the man who was so insistent—so *sure*—on the beach when he proposed to me to make an appearance. To tell me he didn't believe me. Maybe I was hoping for that man to fight so I knew he wouldn't leave, too. Maybe it was even a test.' She lifted a hand to her mouth and he saw it trembling.

But still he couldn't move.

'But that man never showed up, and you failed that test miserably. And still I waited. I *waited* for you to come back to me, Xavier, and tell me that my fears weren't real.' Her gaze was steady on his now. 'I waited three months until I saw the picture of you and Erika on your first date, and then I stopped waiting and realised you weren't that man after all. And that maybe our relationship *had* been childish, and this was the proof I needed to squash my knee-jerk reaction to defend us and claim that it wasn't. So I focused on my kingdom. On what was real and stable. Just like I've been doing for the past few weeks.'

He wanted to tell her it wasn't fair—that pushing him away, expecting him not to accept it, *testing* him, wasn't fair—but his voice wouldn't work.

'You wanted to know, Xavier,' she said, her voice shaking slightly. 'Now you do. I'll head back up and you can follow.' She slid her hand into the pocket he'd put the ring in, and then slid it onto her finger. 'Don't take too long.'

She left him speechless. He knew he didn't have time to process what she'd just told him. Especially not if he considered everything that was swirling around in his head. And now he had to go back up and pretend they were happy together—that all the blame he'd placed on her for ending their relationship hadn't suddenly been shifted to him and hadn't just rocked his entire world.

He relaxed the jaw he'd only just realised he'd clenched and made his way back to the festival. Leyna waited for him just a few metres away from where the guests were gathered, out of their sight, and started walking when he reached her side. They slipped into their royal personas as soon as they were visible, Leyna particularly bubbly as she made her way through the crowds.

He knew she was putting on a show, but he wasn't sure if it was in anticipation of the announcement that needed to be made. She *was* supposed to be a blushing bride after all. The other option was that she, like him, desperately wanted things to go back to the way they'd been before he'd rocked the boat.

When they made their way to where a little stage had been set up to announce the winner, he realised he didn't even know who would win. Not that it mattered, he thought, and clapped along with the crowd at the announcement of the young blonde with the sick husband as the winner.

As the congratulations were made and the photos were taken, he felt nerves skitter through him. He held his breath when the time came for their engagement to be announced, and watched Leyna do it with poise and just the right amount of enthusiasm.

His eyes fluttered over the crowd. He wasn't sure what he'd expected, but the cheers that came a beat after Leyna announced their engagement was definitely not it.

Again, he didn't have time to ponder it. He received the congratulations, posed for the pictures and welcomed everyone to the celebratory ball that evening. It was his only part in the announcement but it exhausted him and by the time they headed back to Aidara's castle Xavier was longing for some privacy.

'Did Carlos speak to you about the arrangements for this evening?' Leyna asked halfway to the castle.

'Yes, he did. They've arranged for me to change in one of the rooms in the east wing.'

'Good.'

Silence followed her words again, and then he heard himself asking, 'Are we going to talk about what happened back there?'

'The engagement?' she asked, her eyes telling him she knew what he was really asking and that the answer was *no*. 'I didn't expect them to react that way,' she continued. 'Did you?'

'I'm not in the mood to play games, Leyna,' he answered tersely.

'I'm not playing a game, Xavier. I'm trying to stay focused on our task. If you'd let me do that from the beginning, we wouldn't have needed this conversation in the first place.'

'How are you so calm about this?' he demanded. 'You just told me something that brings into question everything about the last decade of our lives.'

'No, it doesn't. We've made our choices and now we live with the consequences.' Her face was clear of any emotion. 'We focus on the present. That means we have to convince everyone at tonight's ball that we're happy enough to marry. Can you do that?' she asked very deliberately.

'Yes,' he said through a clenched jaw.

She nodded her head. 'Great.'

The car pulled up in front of the castle then and when Jacob opened her door she moved to get out.

'I'll see you this evening,' she said over her shoulder before leaving the car.

Xavier took a moment to realise he needed to get out, too, and then went directly to the room Carlos had shown him to earlier that morning. He would have liked to go to the gym—*his* gym, to use the punchbag he'd grown used to taking his frustrations out on. But, since that wasn't an option, he poured himself a drink and pushed open the doors to the balcony instead.

He settled in the chair there, resting his legs on the railing as he thought about the mess his life had become over the past weeks. It had started with Zacchaeus, but the convoluted path Xavier and Leyna had taken to deal with that situation hadn't brought them any closer to finding out what Zacchaeus had planned.

It was insurance, yes, but he couldn't help but wonder if they should have tried harder to speak with the King of Kirtida. Perhaps a simple conversation would have clarified things and his life wouldn't have got so complicated.

That was cowardice talking, Xavier told himself. But was it any wonder he wanted to be a coward when being brave had brought him knowledge he should have never pressed for?

Leyna had told him she'd wanted him to fight for her, and he'd *wanted* to. He'd desperately wanted to. But his broken heart had kept him from that in the beginning, and then his family had insisted it was time he moved on and, before he knew it, he was dating and then marrying Erika.

He had to face that part of the reason he'd given in was because he'd been tired of being told what to do. He'd thought that if he gave in to this one thing—this one, massive thing— they would stop. He'd even told himself it wouldn't matter—the only person he'd wanted to marry was Leyna, and since that wasn't happening he might as well give in.

But he'd been a fool. Their judgements about what he did and their opinions about what he should do... It never stopped. In fact, giving in had made them think they had more power. It exhausted him. He'd had to fight to keep Erika happy, he'd had to rule his kingdom *and* he'd had to deal with his mother and grandmother constantly peeking over his shoulder.

No wonder he'd missed the light Leyna had brought to his life.

And perhaps that had been another reason he'd given up on her. His feelings for Leyna had been all-consuming at times, too. His craving for that light had become more and more pressing the older he'd become. In fact, on the day he'd proposed to her, when he'd told her she wanted to escape her royal duties to spend time with him, he had been doing that very thing with *her*.

When she'd broken his heart she'd broken it completely. And so, with his father's reminder about his responsibilities, perhaps it had been easier to accept what they'd wanted him to do.

Perhaps he hadn't wanted to fight for her so hard after all…

He downed the drink and set the glass back on the ground. He'd so badly hoped Leyna hadn't been right. Especially since her words made his heart ache. But paying attention to that pain would mean so much more than facing the fact that he hadn't wanted to fight for her. No, admitting it also forced him to accept what he hadn't wanted to in the last ten years—that he hadn't given his marriage all of himself.

It crushed him. He set his feet back down and rested his head in his hands. His family's expectations of him might have been unrealistic at times, but perhaps in disappointing them it had been a bad omen for the future.

He'd disappointed Leyna by not coming back and, though it might not have been fair of her to expect him to, he agreed that their years together meant she might have expected him to try. He'd disappointed Erika by not being the husband she deserved—not only in what he'd offered her of himself, but by being unable to give her a child, too.

He didn't think that feeling could be topped until he realised that he was disappointed in himself, too. And *that* was perhaps the worst of them all.

* * *

She'd fallen back into the honesty that had once come so naturally between them.

That was the only reason Leyna could think of to explain why she'd told him something she'd only just discovered herself. Perhaps it was because of all the not thinking—and then the inevitable thinking—she'd been doing over the last days. And when she'd finally allowed it to come to her consciousness, the realisations had come spilling out of her mouth.

The reason they had spilled out to Xavier could only be because she'd been lulled into a false sense of security by remembering what they'd once shared. There wasn't any other reason—none that would make her feel confident in her decision to marry him and carry his child, that was.

So, instead, she thought about what she'd told Xavier. It was so clear to her now that she'd been afraid of losing him. It made sense to her, too. More than any other reason she'd given herself for making that decision. In the years following it, she couldn't think of one reason why she'd done it. She'd regretted it, had felt a knife twist in her heart every time she'd seen Xavier and Erika together—a reminder that *she'd* been the one to push him away.

But now she knew that she'd needed time.

More importantly, she'd needed him to tell her that he wouldn't leave. That they could rule together without losing sight of who—and why—they were ruling. She'd been young, she'd had her entire life thrown on its head with her father's death.

She reminded herself of that when she felt accusation claw at her. When her thoughts filled with how much she'd hurt him.

If she didn't remind herself of it, she'd spend her life struggling to forgive herself. And she didn't want to live like that.

Would she struggle to forgive him, too? she wondered, starting the ritual of getting ready for the ball. She'd always told herself she'd been hurt because he'd moved on so quickly to Erika. Now she knew she'd really been hurt that he'd moved on at all.

She smiled at the ladies who'd helped her get ready for events all her life, but her mind wandered as she let them do their work. She felt…lighter at the realisation. It settled something that had been brooding inside her for so long.

The feeling made her think that she *would* forgive Xavier. That maybe she already had. And that the tightness in her chest as she made her way to the ballroom was because she needed to ask him for his forgiveness, too.

Maybe it would finally help them both to move on. To build their future without hurt being part of their foundation.

And then she forgot about all of it as she stood at the top of the stairs and saw Xavier waiting for her at the bottom.

She'd thought it the night of the banquet, too, but then she hadn't really allowed herself to enjoy seeing Xavier in his uniform that night. Though she wasn't sure what had changed, she was glad it had. He was strikingly handsome, his hair combed back in a style that made it all the more obvious. The uniform fitted him perfectly—suited him, too—and, though it didn't reveal much of his body, knowing the muscular shape of it sent a slow thrill through her.

Their eyes met and lit a fire across the staircase. Her body heated from it—from the fire she saw reflecting in his eyes as she made her way down—and she was afraid that she would go up in flames when she finally stopped in front of him.

'People might suspect that our child isn't a honeymoon baby if you keep looking at me like that,' she said huskily as she slid her arm into the one he offered.

'You shouldn't have worn that dress then, Your Majesty.'

She looked down at the off-the-shoulder burgundy dress that only really revealed her shoulders. 'This dress is perfectly acceptable.'

'Sure it is,' he said softly as they approached the ballroom. 'For one purpose.' He glanced down at her and his eyes told her exactly what he thought that purpose was. She blushed and then put on a smile as they were announced in the hall.

If she had to judge how her people felt about her engagement based on the ball that evening she had nothing to worry about. And though she received comments that told her some guessed the real motivation for their marriage, they were all supportive. And usually accompanied with some form of 'It's about time' remark.

They gave the proper honour to the winner of the festival, too, and before she knew it dinner had come and gone and she and Xavier were opening the party on the dance floor. Her body braced as he placed his hand on her waist, and as she placed hers on his shoulder while the other took his hand she felt his body tighten, too.

'Relax,' she whispered when the music started, and she forced herself to take heed of the instruction just as she felt Xavier did. It helped, but didn't lessen the tension between them. She relaxed slightly when the other couples joined them, and forced herself to release an unsteady breath.

'I take it you'll be returning to Mattan this evening,' she said to focus her mind on something else.

'That would probably be for the best.'

'You're welcome to stay, though.' She smiled as the festival winner and her husband—who looked healthier than Leyna had seen him in a while—passed them in a twirl, and then directed her gaze at Xavier. 'You're always welcome here.'

Something softened in his eyes, but he shook his head. 'It wouldn't be a good idea for me to stay here. But thank you for the offer.'

She nodded, and told herself it was for the best. She was preparing herself to return to mingle when the next song came on, and felt her breath catch when Xavier pulled her in until their bodies were moulded to one another.

'I don't think people will mind thinking our child was conceived out of wedlock,' Xavier told her a few moments later.

'Of course you don't,' she replied, fighting to keep her tone light. 'If you did, you wouldn't be looking at me like we will be conceiving the baby as soon as we leave the room.'

He gave a small laugh. 'I could probably turn it down a notch.'

'You should,' she agreed. 'You're good at that, too.'

She felt his body stiffen, and shifted her gaze so she didn't have to look into the eyes that saw too much. 'You know why I did that, Leyna. It wasn't because I didn't want you.'

'Wasn't it?' she asked, keeping her tone light. 'You don't have to explain it. I know you were married and that—' she struggled with her next words '—you and I aren't on the same page any more.'

'And that, to you, means that I don't want you?'

'Wanting someone physically and wanting them emotionally isn't the same thing, Xavier.'

'I know that,' he said, his voice strangled. 'And somehow you've got it into your head that I only want you in one of those ways?'

'You loved Erika. I don't blame you for not wanting to—' she cleared her throat '—tarnish that by…by making love with me.'

'That's what you think?' Something in his tone had her looking up at him, and she nodded. He didn't reply and they swayed together, a weight she'd never expected settling between them. When the song was done she put distance between them, looking up in surprise when Xavier didn't let go of her hand.

'Come with me,' he said, half-plea, half-command. She nodded and followed him to the door where Carlos stood. Xavier whispered something into her secretary's ear and, without expression, Carlos nodded and bowed to them both.

Leyna followed Xavier helplessly then, holding her breath when she realised he was leading her through the secret tunnels that went to the beach.

To their place.

She shook her head, cautioning herself not to go there. She watched him grab the blanket that was always at the door and went outside with him, only stopping before they hit the sand.

'I'm not going down to the beach in a *ball-gown*,' she said, exasperated. 'Especially not if we're going back to the ball.'

'We're not,' he answered, taking his jacket off. Her eyes greedily took in the muscles that were clear in the white T-shirt he'd worn under his uniform jacket, and then she forced them back to his face.

'What do you mean, *we're not*?'

'I mean I told Carlos we wouldn't be returning.' He dropped to take off his shoes, and then started on hers. She gasped when she felt her feet leave the shoes as he scooped her into his arms, the blanket now over his shoulders.

'Wh…what are you doing?'

'I'm saving you the time it would have taken to tell me you couldn't ruin a dress made with such effort and expertise by walking through the sand.'

'So you thought you'd treat me like a cave-man would?'

'When's the last time you saw a movie or read a book? This is romantic.'

'I beg to differ,' she said, though, in all honesty, she *did* think it was a little romantic. Not because of the action, but because of the motivation behind it. He was being thoughtful as she *would* have worried about ruining her beautiful dress, and *that* was pretty romantic.

Being alone on the beach under the stars didn't hurt, either.

But then he stopped, and she could almost see the smoke coming from his ears as he tried to figure out how he would get the blanket from his shoulders to the ground.

She laughed. 'How about I help with that, Mr Romance?'

'Thanks,' he said with a sheepish smile and, though awkwardly, somehow they managed to spread the blanket on the ground and she sat down without touching the sand. He joined her then, settling on his back with his arms behind his head. She caught a glimpse of toned flesh as his T-shirt crept up, and she quickly lay on her back beside him, carefully placing her hands on her belly to ensure one of them didn't somehow land on the skin she'd just seen.

'I doubt this is going to go down very well. The hosts of an engagement party leaving before their guests do.'

'They'll get over it,' Xavier said easily. She turned her head and saw him take a deep breath. 'I needed this.'

'To escape?' she asked softly, and he smiled.

'I'm not sure we can ever escape. Not really. Our guards probably had us surrounded the moment we came down here.'

'So this is as good as it's ever going to get,' she replied and took a deep breath of her own. 'From where I am, I don't think it gets better.'

'You're just saying that because this is your favourite place. Or was,' he added quickly.

'It still is.'

'I should have known when I found you here after the State Banquet.'

'I have only good memories here,' she told him and then shook her head. 'Mostly.'

Silence followed her words, though, for some reason, Leyna didn't find it tense. She kept her eyes on the stars twinkling down on her, reminding her of the beauty in the world.

And, though she would probably regret

thinking it later, she enjoyed being there with him. It felt a little like that day when both the best and worst thing had happened to her. But now she was here and she'd survived them both.

'Do you regret it?' he asked suddenly. 'Saying yes to me?'

Her heart gave an uncomfortable thud in her chest. 'No.'

'Not even now, knowing what you know?'

'No,' she said again, and took a deep breath to prepare herself for what she knew she had to say next. 'I do regret the way I ended it, though. I regret hurting you as much as I did.' She inhaled and used the breath to say the words she should have said that afternoon. 'I'm sorry, Xavier. I truly am sorry for hurting you.'

'And I'm sorry for not fighting for you,' he replied softly. She turned her head to look at him. 'You were right. I should have.'

'But it was unfair of me to expect it from you.' Emotion, thick and heavy, sat in her throat. 'I didn't know that I had expected it, not until I told you so this afternoon. But I was young, and afraid, and—'

'Fear doesn't always make us think rationally.'

'No, it doesn't.'

She looked away, afraid the emotion of the

moment would make her cry again. It was ridiculous, even having the urge, but she supposed that was only to be expected. She'd kept everything about that time in a box, shut tight, refusing to let it make her any less of a queen.

And maybe she'd managed to keep it locked for so long because she hadn't had anyone to share it with. Until now, it seemed.

'My family wanted me to marry Erika.'

The unexpected words had her head whipping to look at him again. 'What?'

'They realised that whatever had happened between us hadn't been a simple tiff and insisted I move on. So I did.'

She opened her mouth, and then closed it again. When she was sure she could speak without giving away her emotions, she asked, 'So, you only dated her because they told you to?'

'That's what I thought, yes. Until this afternoon. And then I realised maybe it had been easier to listen to them than to face possible rejection from you again. I don't think my heart would have been able to take it a second time.'

Her mind spun with the information, and she heard herself asking him about his marriage. 'So how did you decide that you would date Erika?'

'She was the daughter of one of my father's

advisers. She'd been doing humanitarian work, had a good reputation in the influential circles of Mattan, and my mother and grandmother thought she was a suitable match. My father did, too.'

'Was it…arranged?'

'Not in the way you mean.' He shifted his body so he was on his side, looking at her. 'It was a *suggested* marriage. And I'd already wasted the year after my twenty-first birthday—in their opinion—waiting for you.' He fell silent.

'I don't think any of them believed in love. My grandmother had chosen my mother for my father to marry, and they'd grown to care about each other over the years. I don't think they knew how it felt to love someone like…' His voice faded, and she saw the hesitation in his eyes before he continued. 'I don't think they knew what it was to feel what I felt for you.'

Her heart broke and not for the first time she found herself wishing she could go back. That she could stop herself throwing away the love Xavier had had for her. That she could stop herself hurting him as badly as she clearly had, denying herself the chance to be loved.

'Did you try to tell them?'

'What was the use?' He shook his head. 'I

didn't think you loved me, and that would have been the only motivation. Besides, I was devastated. And I can see now that moving on with Erika… It was an expectation. A command, even, from my King. I couldn't disobey him. I had no reason to.'

She understood it, even if it broke her heart even more.

'So I listened to them and I married, because that's what a king has to do.' He shrugged in a way that told her his family had reminded him of that fact as well.

'And Erika was fine with that?'

'She didn't entirely have the option not to be. She had a father who wanted her to marry into the royal family, and a king who expected her to marry his son. How could she refuse?'

'So you *both* didn't want to be in the relationship?'

'I didn't say that.'

'I thought…' She faltered. 'I'm sorry, I just can't imagine being in a relationship because that's what people told me I should do.'

'Is that why you haven't dated since us?'

She gave a soft laugh. 'Walked straight into that one, didn't I?' But, because he'd been honest with her, she would give him the same courtesy. 'Yes, I think so. I've always known that I would have to marry one day. But I was postponing it for as long as I could. Despite the urges of my grandmother.'

'She wanted you to marry?'

'In the same way your family wanted you to move on. She concocted the most outlandish ways to get men she thought appropriate in front of me without saying that she wanted me to meet them. At first,' Leyna added, thinking about recent years. 'But then she gave up and started telling me outright that I couldn't be a spinster queen. That I needed to give Aidara a future ruler.'

'And even that didn't sway you?'

'It should have, but...' She trailed off, her mind spinning a bit at the prospect. 'It *has* now, though, hasn't it?' she said, instead of what she really thought.

That perhaps duty hadn't dictated *every* decision of her personal life. And what did it mean that she'd let it do so now? With Xavier?

'See, I told you that you were stronger—better—than I was.'

'Because I didn't marry when my grandmother told me to?' she scoffed. 'That's hardly something to be proud of.'

'I disagree,' he said softly. 'Maybe if I'd done the same, she wouldn't have—' He broke off.

'She wouldn't have what?'

He shook his head, rolling onto his back again. 'It's nothing.'

She pushed up onto her forearms. 'It isn't nothing, Xavier, or you wouldn't have brought it up. What did you want to say?'

'It's nothing,' he repeated stubbornly.

'Is it nothing?' she asked, trying a different tactic. 'Or is it just something that you don't want to share with me?'

'Don't make this about you, Leyna.'

'But it is, though, isn't it? What else could it possibly be about?'

'Erika,' he snapped. 'My wife. The woman I should have protected.'

CHAPTER TEN

XAVIER'S CHEST WAS heaving and he closed his eyes, fighting for calm. Leyna's hand closed over his and it helped steady his breath. But he couldn't keep the contact when he was talking about Erika and he pulled his hand away, settling it on his chest.

When he opened his eyes again, he pretended not to see the hurt on her face or how she sat up, the ease that had her lying on her back gone.

'What should you have protected her from?' Leyna asked quietly, turning away from him. He sat up now, too, and felt the guilt at hurting her throb in his chest.

'I shouldn't have brought it up.'

'But you did, so clearly some part of you wanted to talk about it.'

'Or you pushed so hard that I had no choice.'

She gave a soft bark of laughter. 'If it helps you to blame me, then by all means go ahead.'

She pushed up to her knees and Xavier got to his feet to help her up. She let him, but let go of his hand the moment she was standing.

He couldn't blame her, and shouldn't have let it bother him. Yet he felt the same hurt that she'd had in her eyes when he'd let go of her hand minutes ago.

'Can you take me back?' she asked, not looking at him.

'Leyna—'

'Can you just take me back, please?' she asked sharply now.

He sighed and lifted her into his arms, thinking about how different things had been just a few moments ago. He was responsible for that, he thought. He needed to face the truth of that—that he so easily blamed her without taking responsibility himself.

Something he was beginning to realise happened more and more.

So when they reached the path to the castle and he set her back on her feet he opened his mouth to apologise, but was silenced when she spoke.

'We need boundaries,' she said, slipping her feet back into the heels she'd worn. 'Things we shouldn't talk about because it would undermine the cordiality we'd like to maintain in our relationship.' She straightened. 'I think

I already know what's on your list and, since we've cleared the air about what happened ten years ago, I'd like to add our past to that, too.'

'You think we can avoid talking about our past?' he asked in disbelief.

'We must if we want to keep this marriage as civil as possible.'

'And that's essential, isn't it?' he said, hiding his anger. But he should have known that she'd see through it.

'You don't get to be angry with me when you're the one who put up walls. Perhaps you didn't say it—' she cut off his protest '—but not wanting to talk about it, snapping at me when I ask you to, that's a wall. And I refuse to feel...' Her voice faded and he saw a flash of hurt on her face. 'I don't want us to take our anger out on each other any more. So—' she straightened her shoulders '—can I count on you for that?'

'Yes,' he replied a little helplessly.

'Then I'll say goodnight. I'll have Carlos let you know when the results of the pregnancy test are in.'

She walked away from him then, leaving him speechless. It occurred to him that it wasn't the first time she'd done it that day, and he was beginning to wonder whether that was how she dealt with difficult situations.

But then, he knew that wasn't true. She'd faced *their* situation—which in optimistic terms could be described as difficult—head-on, with the strength and grace he'd come to expect from her as Queen. Perhaps then it was Leyna the woman, not Leyna the Queen, who walked away from difficult situations. And perhaps it wasn't so much the situation as it was the person.

Him.

He couldn't blame her, he thought. He'd lashed out and let his emotions get the better of him. But it felt wrong talking to Leyna about Erika. About what he should have done for Erika.

Because if he told her why he'd needed to protect Erika, what was there to stop him from telling her that he'd needed to love his wife more, too? That he'd needed to give up the hope that he'd somehow still carried for him and Leyna—even though he'd been *married*—and put his wife first?

He'd been avoiding telling Leyna what his mistakes were because his biggest one had partly been because of her. And how could he tell her that? How could he admit that out loud? He had enough trouble facing it himself, let alone validating its existence by telling her about it.

His dilemma was that she was the only one he'd ever been comfortable talking about it with. He sighed, wondering, not for the first time, how his life had become such a mess.

The next morning he found out.

He'd got the news that Zacchaeus had positioned a fleet of ships off Kirtida's shores as soon as it happened. Less than an hour later, Xavier was alone with Leyna in his library after being briefed on the latest developments.

'So, one of the ships from that fleet is on its way here,' Xavier said. 'I can only imagine it's Zacchaeus.'

'Who else could it be?' she agreed. 'And if it is, his timing is interesting.'

'Right after our engagement announcement.' Xavier nodded. 'I think our plan might be working.'

'Or it could be backfiring,' Leyna said. 'We were told his ships could be in position to either attack or defend. At this point, we don't know which is more likely.'

'I suppose you're right.' Xavier thought about it and then said, 'He's on his way to Mattan, though. Why?'

'Because he doesn't know that I'm here and he wants to offer *you* a proposition.'

'Whatever it is, I'm not interested.'

'Of course you aren't,' she said dryly. 'Or else this—' she wiggled the fingers on her left hand, making the engagement ring glint at him '—would have been moot.'

'I couldn't exactly go to Zacchaeus and ask *him* for his hand in marriage as part of an alliance,' Xavier replied sarcastically, and felt some of the tension that had settled at the pit of his belly dissolve when she laughed.

'You're right,' she said in mock seriousness.

'That's the only thing keeping me on your side, Your Majesty,' he said with a smile of his own. They stayed like that for a moment, smiling at each other as though the threat to their kingdoms wasn't on his way to see them.

Leyna was the first to snap out of it. 'We're going to have to make an announcement to our people after this. They've been waiting for it, and I don't think we'll be able to delay any longer. Especially considering that our fleet will have to respond.'

'You're right.' Xavier sat opposite her. 'What will we say?'

'That our diplomatic attempts with Kirtida have failed, and that Zacchaeus is no longer interested in being a part of the Alliance of the Three Isles.'

'They might not be in the mood for a wedding after that.'

'Perhaps,' she considered. 'Or perhaps they'll be thrilled because we'll tell them that the wedding will assure the alliance of our two kingdoms and therefore keep them safe.'

His thoughts once again went to how strong, how graceful a queen she was, but he kept them to himself. Considering her words, he said, 'What does it say about me that I'm hoping we can resolve all of this right now with Zacchaeus?'

'It says you'd like to avoid the disaster of a possible war for the sake of your people.' Her expression went from serious to soft. 'It's not a weakness to want to solve this without violence, Xavier.'

'It feels like it.'

'Then we're both weak.' Her gaze stayed on his, and he wasn't sure what she saw there that had her nodding. 'You know, we have a trump card in this discussion.'

'Which is?' She laid a hand on her belly and his chest suddenly tightened. 'You want to tell him about the *baby*?'

'Don't make it sound like an unreasonable suggestion.'

'But…we don't even know if it's a reality yet.'

'We don't have to know. All we have to do

is convince *him* of it, which might have him thinking twice about going into war.'

'Why?' Xavier asked, the emotion he couldn't identify that was churning in him making the words fierce. Bitter. 'Because an unborn child is going to tap into his compassionate side?'

'No.' Her eyes flashed with annoyance. 'Because it means that Aidara and Mattan are unequivocally and irrevocably linked.'

'Is there nothing sacred to you?' he snapped. 'Or is everything just leverage? In the name of duty?'

He read the emotions that sped across her face like a book he hated but couldn't put down. Shock. Indignation. Hurt. He braced himself when anger finally settled, but there was no chance for her to tell him how he'd made her feel. Not when Xavier got the call telling him Zacchaeus had arrived and was on his way up.

He could see that Leyna knew what the phone call had been about and she walked onto his balcony, the summer breeze tousling her hair. He ran a hand through his own and contemplated going out to her to apologise. But he wasn't sure what he would be apologising for, and thought that the anger still sizzling in his stomach might actually be useful for the conversation they were about to have.

A knock at the door edged that anger with nerves. He heard Leyna enter the room again and straightened his shoulders as he called for their guest to come in.

'King Zacchaeus is here, Your Majesty,' his private secretary announced and quickly closed the door behind her.

'Zacchaeus,' Xavier said when he saw the dark-haired man he'd once considered an ally. 'We weren't expecting you.'

'And I hadn't expected a "we",' Zacchaeus answered, his brown eyes settling on Leyna.

Xavier felt jealousy coil inside him when he saw the appreciation in Zacchaeus' eyes, and forced himself to ignore it. Zacchaeus was baiting him, the logical side of him knew. And it was smart, he thought, when Zacchaeus' eyes settled on him again with a glint that told Xavier it was strategy.

'There's always a "we", Zacchaeus,' Leyna said. 'That "we" used to include you and your kingdom. Are you here to clarify whether that's still the case?'

'I'm here to offer my congratulations,' Zacchaeus said easily. 'I must say I feel partially responsible for you two finally getting together.'

'Oh, you're entirely responsible,' Xavier answered in the same tone. 'But, if we're all being honest here, you already knew that.'

'Yes.' The answer was curt, Zacchaeus' bantering tone gone. 'And it's disheartening to see Kirtida's allies act as a duet as opposed to a trio.'

'That tends to happen when a member of a three-way alliance removes themselves from the alliance,' Leyna said.

'That's not entirely true, though,' Zacchaeus answered, and something behind his guarded expression had Xavier wondering what was happening with the new King of Kirtida.

'What would you call refusing to answer our requests for a meeting then?' Xavier asked, keeping his eyes steady on Zacchaeus' face. 'What would you call refusing to *see* us when we arrived at Kirtida to talk about the future of our alliance?'

'Complicated,' Zacchaeus answered.

'If this is some kind of game to you, Zacchaeus, we're not interested,' Leyna said. 'All we'd like to know is whether you're formally withdrawing from the alliance. If you aren't, then we can use this opportunity to discuss the agreement, since you seem unfamiliar with its terms.'

Zacchaeus' expression darkened at her words

but Leyna continued. 'And if you are, then we should discuss the legalities of that, too. Either way, this meeting will be productive.'

'You know I've always liked you, Leyna,' Zacchaeus told her, his eyes lit with admiration. Although he wasn't sure, Xavier thought it was genuine. 'Respected you, too. And, in honour of that, I'll be as honest with you as you are with me.'

Xavier doubted that, but he kept silent and watched as Zacchaeus shoved his hands into his pockets. For a moment, Xavier caught a glimpse of the man he'd known growing up. But when he looked at them again, Zacchaeus' eyes were harder, darker, and Xavier knew not to make the mistake of thinking he was the man he'd once appeared to be.

'Contrary to your belief, Leyna, I *am* aware of the terms of the alliance. I might not have ruled for as long as either of you have, but that doesn't mean I'm a novice,' Zacchaeus said grimly. 'I knew what it would mean when I chose not to attend the Banquet.'

'You intended it,' Leyna said, and something flashed across his face—could it have been uncertainty?—before he replied.

'Now you both understand how serious I am about what I'm here to discuss.'

'What *are* you here to discuss, Zacchaeus?' Xavier interjected.

Zacchaeus' face went blank, except for the seriousness in his eyes. 'We need to renegotiate the terms of the alliance. Or there will be no alliance at all.'

CHAPTER ELEVEN

THOUGH SHE'D EXPECTED the words the moment she'd heard about Zacchaeus' fleet, Leyna's chest constricted at the confirmation. She felt the insidious pulse of panic throb with each heartbeat and fought to keep it from showing on her face.

Instead, she focused on the fact that she wasn't supposed to have been there at all, and the indignation that came with that realisation.

'You intended on renegotiating the terms of the alliance without me?' she forced herself to say lightly. 'I'm not sure if you meant for me to be insulted, Zacchaeus, but you've certainly achieved it.'

'When I heard about your engagement, Leyna, I assumed Xavier would tell you everything that I told him.'

'But there's more.'

'Yes,' Zacchaeus allowed. 'If he had agreed to renegotiating the terms when it had been only the two of us, I would have wanted assurances that Kirtida's part of the alliance would be just as strong as Mattan's and Aidara's. Unfortunately, you can't help with that.'

Her mind quickly pieced it together, but Xavier started to ask what Zacchaeus meant and then stopped when realisation dawned on him. Horror, lined with a fear she'd never seen him show before, passed across his face, but was quickly replaced by a carefully blank expression.

'Is that why your ships have been readied?' Xavier asked, his voice dangerously low. 'To intimidate us into negotiating with you? To intimidate me into offering you *my sister*?'

'They were readied for the same reason yours will be as soon as I leave here, I imagine,' Zacchaeus responded. 'That is why this discussion is so important.'

'Which terms do you want to renegotiate?' Leyna asked quickly. She wasn't sure Xavier would able to speak without provoking Zacchaeus.

'The Protection of the Alliance of the Three Isles.'

'What about it?'

'I need assurance that should Kirtida be involved in a…disagreement, its allies would step in and support the action.'

'That's what the agreement currently states,'

Leyna replied, and then she frowned. 'But since you're here, specifically mentioning this, there's clearly a loophole that doesn't cover your particular kind of disagreement.'

'We need protection from every country, Leyna.' Zacchaeus' eyes were more sombre than she'd ever seen them.

'Again, that *is* the purpose of the Protection of the Alliance...' Leyna trailed off. 'You mean with one of our allies? With the alliance's allies?'

'Yes.'

It suddenly made sense, she thought. He hadn't come to the banquet because he might have had to face the ally he was requesting protection from.

The pulse of panic slipped into her blood, coursing through her veins, becoming harder to ignore. She swallowed, and begged her body to give her more time.

'We can't agree to that,' Xavier said, his eyes moving from Leyna—where it flashed with concern—to Zacchaeus. He seemed to have put his feelings about Zacchaeus' implication aside. 'It could undermine *all* of our international relationships.'

'Perhaps it's time to forge new ones.'

'Zacchaeus, this isn't something you can just decide on the spur of the moment,' Leyna said, finding her voice again. 'It takes thought, reasoning, negotiation. You've been King for a month and you already want to jump into this?'

'Does this sound like something I *want* to jump into, Leyna?' Zacchaeus snapped. 'There are factors at play here that—' He cut himself off, clenching his jaw. 'Regardless of how long I've been King, I *am* responsible for Kirtida. And this is what is necessary to ensure that my kingdom is protected.'

'What have you done, Zacchaeus?' Xavier asked. 'Tell us what's happened to make this such a necessity.'

Leyna saw the conflict in Zacchaeus' eyes before he cleared them of emotion. 'That's not possible. Not now. I understand you might need some time to think this through, but I'd like you to consider this. We're stronger as three than as one. If I withdraw from the alliance—'

'There'll be two of us and one of you?' Xavier asked, and Leyna saw Zacchaeus' jaw tighten once more.

'There'll be conflict,' Zacchaeus replied. 'It would be better for that conflict not to be within an alliance that spans centuries.'

He was out of the door as soon as the words had left his mouth, leaving a stunned silence behind.

Leyna lowered herself onto the couch, forcing air into her lungs as she closed her eyes. She prayed that Xavier would give her a moment to regain control, but she didn't check to see whether that was the case. She was painfully aware of her stomach, her heart, her chest—and she just wanted them to relax again.

She gave herself a few minutes and then opened her eyes when she felt steadier. Xavier sat across from her, his face carefully blank.

'Are you okay?'

'I'm fine,' she replied, feeling her cheeks heat. 'I just needed a moment.'

He nodded and got up to pour her a glass of water. 'Is it possible that this is a side-effect—'

'Of pregnancy?' She took the water from him and watched him sit down again as she took a sip. 'No. There should still be some time before the symptoms show up. *If* I'm pregnant. Besides, it's happened before.'

'And what exactly is *it*?'

'Anxiety.'

Now, she felt the colour seep from her cheeks. She didn't want Xavier to know about the panic attacks she'd started having after her mother had left. They'd been much, much worse in the past but each episode—regardless of its intensity—left her feeling so incredibly vulnerable and fragile.

She'd put those days behind her, developed strategies to cope. She hadn't had one—the kind that had had her bodyguards develop a protocol for them anyway—in years. The dreams, like the one she'd had the other day, came and went, but not the panic attacks. It felt awful that she'd come so close in recent weeks.

Just as she had before, she would cope.

But she didn't want to share that with him.

'You shouldn't have to deal with it alone,' Xavier said, interrupting her thoughts.

'With my anxiety?' she asked, shaking her head. 'It's not exactly the kind of thing you can share with other people.'

'Sometimes it is.'

'Not in our position.'

'But now we have each other.'

Her heart stalled at the words, but she accepted them, telling herself this was all part of the cordiality they'd agreed to the night before. She nodded. 'Yes, we do. So let's talk about what we're going to do about Zacchaeus.'

It felt good to finally discuss the situation in the light of new information. Not that it was positive, Leyna thought, telling Xavier as much. They didn't have many options. On the one hand, they could refuse to negotiate with Zacchaeus. But they didn't know what trouble he was in, or how it would impact Mattan and Aidara.

On the other hand, they *could* negotiate with him, and be impacted by that trouble willingly. But that might also entail a marriage between Nalini and Zacchaeus, which neither of them were willing to decide on.

'You could talk to her,' Leyna said. 'Leave it completely up to her.'

'And tell her what? That the future of Mattan is in her hands?'

'Of course not. The future of Mattan is in *our* hands. But how are we going to make a decision about *either* of our kingdoms without knowing what *all* of our options are?'

'If Nalini *did* agree to marry Zacchaeus, how would that help us decide on what to do?'

'I know this is hard, Xavier.' Leyna resisted the urge to lean forward, to grip his hand with hers. *Boundaries.* 'But we have to make some kind of decision. And, based on Zacchaeus' reaction, we won't have very long to make it.'

'If we don't negotiate with him, we have war between the Isles *and* a possible external threat. We'll break a centuries-long alliance and threaten the trust of our people, putting their lives at risk.' He got up and poured himself a drink now. 'If we do, we have *no* war between the Isles, face a *possible* external threat, and my sister has to marry the man who's put us in this situation in the first place.'

'Those are our options,' Leyna confirmed, her gaze staying on him. She waited for what she knew—what she'd feared—would come next.

'If we'd just waited before doing all of this, we might not have been in this situation.'

'We *did* wait, Xavier,' Leyna said, forcing coolness into her tone. 'And you know our actions are the reason Zacchaeus was here in the first place. Why he was willing to talk about this at all.'

And because it was easier to pre-empt, she said, 'In my view, our best option is to talk to Zacchaeus about the protection clause in the alliance agreement. But we'll ask him for a week to consider it before we tell him that we've made a decision.'

'Why?'

'Because we'll find out whether I'm pregnant in a week.' She went on, needing to accept the finality of her words, 'If I'm not, we go to Zacchaeus as equals—all three of us. Nalini won't have to marry Zacchaeus and—'

'You mean break off our engagement?' She nodded. 'So you get to break up with me all over again.'

'There's nothing to break up, Xavier,' she

said, ignoring the emotion inside her that screamed the contrary. 'And you can't deny that you were looking for a way out. I'm offering you one. So, if I'm not pregnant, you'll protect your sister and we'll protect our kingdoms.'

She didn't wait for a reply, leaving the room—leaving his company—so she could catch her breath again. The panic wouldn't be as easily abated this time, she thought, which had the tension in her chest increasing.

She escaped as far as she could away from the library, hoping no one would see her. But with each step the pressure grew, eventually causing her to stop and press her back against the nearest wall.

She didn't know how long she stood there, nor did she care. All she knew was that her head suddenly felt as if it were on a roundabout and her lungs felt as if they were burning.

'Leyna.'

She nearly groaned when she heard Xavier's voice, but instead opened her eyes. 'I just need a few moments.'

'And you can have them,' Xavier answered softly. 'In private.'

'Okay,' she replied, but couldn't bring herself to move. After a few seconds, Xavier sighed and scooped her into his arms just as easily as he had the night before.

'You don't have to do this,' she said automatically.

'No, apparently, I do,' he said in strained annoyance.

She didn't see where he took her and only realised she was in his bedroom when he laid her on the bed. She rested her head against the pillows and watched him open the windows. The sea air immediately filled the room, stilling some of the spinning in her head.

'Why do you insist on doing this to yourself?'

'It's not a choice.'

He started to pace. 'Fine, but I thought you were going to let me help you.'

'How can I let you help when you're the one making me feel this way?'

He stopped. 'I make you anxious?'

'Yes. No.' She sighed. 'I don't know if it's you or the situation.'

'Both, probably,' he said, and lowered himself next to her on the bed. 'How can I make it better?'

'You can't. Not unless you can go back to the past and change everything I did to ruin us.' She was tired, she thought, and blamed that for the slip. 'I'm sorry, I shouldn't have...' She shook her head. 'Boundaries.'

'I didn't agree with that idea then and I don't agree with it now.'

'Really? So you want to keep going back over the past like a broken record? Because that's what it feels like, Xavier. And I can't stop listening to the stupid record because every time I see you it plays on repeat.'

'Then let it,' he said, and turned towards her. 'Let it play.'

'And what would that achieve? What would replaying that hurt, those mistakes, possibly achieve?'

'It'll remind us of what we need to stay away from in the future.'

'Why, Xavier? There is no future for us. There can't be. Not when so much has happened.'

He didn't reply immediately, and she could hear emotion in his voice when he spoke, though she couldn't identify it. 'Is that why you have the dreams, the anxiety attacks?'

'No, those come from ruling a kingdom by myself with no support.'

'But having no support is because of the choices, the *mistakes* you've made, isn't it?'

Realising what he was doing, she moved to the opposite end of the bed from where he sat and set her feet on the ground. '*This* was a mistake. I shouldn't have said anything.'

'It wasn't a mistake, Leyna.' He got off the bed, turned to face her. 'It was you finally being honest with yourself.'

She let out a bitter laugh. 'I *am* being honest with myself. I'm facing the fact that this marriage isn't something you want, let alone this child. Or maybe it is, but just not with me. You moved on, remember?' she said before he could protest. 'And you were so reluctant to go ahead with this plan.'

'This was *my* plan, Leyna. Getting married was *my* suggestion.'

'Because your kingdom was in danger!' Leyna knew she should leave but something wouldn't let her. 'You had years to salvage our relationship.'

'So did you!'

'And how would I do that? Come to see you and *your wife* and tell you that I'd made a terrible mistake and that I still loved you?'

CHAPTER TWELVE

'*LOVED*,' LEYNA SAID in a voice just as stunned as the expression on her face. 'I said loved. Past tense.'

'When did you stop loving me?' Xavier asked, ignoring the voice that warned him not to.

'When you got married to someone else.'

'But you said that you would have had to tell me *and* Erika that you still loved me. Which would mean you still loved me when I was married.'

'I was talking about when you two were dating,' Leyna said, though he heard the desperation in her tone. 'Why does it matter?' She didn't wait for an answer. 'We have enough to deal with in our present, Xavier. And in our future. We don't have to keep going back to the past.' She gave him a beseeching look. 'Okay?'

He wanted to say no. He wanted to get to the bottom of what she'd just admitted to him.

But his eyes fluttered to the bedside table near where she stood. A picture of Erika smiled back at him, and he felt emotion seize his vocal cords.

He saw her eyes follow his and when she looked back at him they told him she knew he wouldn't argue with her.

'I'll call you in a week, once I get the test results,' Leyna said, none of the angst they'd shared in the last minutes evident in her voice. 'We can decide what to do then.' She walked to the door. 'I'll tell Zacchaeus we need the time. I don't think he'll be a real threat until we've made a decision, but I'll get his assurances. You can talk to Nalini. It'll be best if we know where she stands when the time comes.'

And then she was gone, and Xavier could no longer ignore the feelings tumbling through him. He walked to the picture of Erika and picked it up, wondering how she still had so much control over him three years after her death.

Perhaps it was because he hadn't given her what she'd deserved when she was alive. And perhaps he was just using *that* as an excuse to ignore that he'd started feeling something for Leyna again. He *needed* an excuse to face that. To somehow mute the voice that told him he was making a mistake.

Fool me once, shame on you. Fool me twice...

But he'd felt a real, visceral fear when she'd given him the option to back out. And he'd known why she'd done it. Just like ten years before, she was making a decision *for* him. To protect herself from anticipating it in the future. And though that made him wonder why she thought she needed to protect herself—especially if, as she claimed, there were no feelings involved—that fear remained.

But he couldn't deny that her offer had been tempting—which was probably why he hadn't called her out on what she was doing. His life would go back to what it had been. Yes, there would be the complication of Zacchaeus, and whatever had prompted this entire situation. But he wouldn't have to marry Leyna and be reminded of a life he shouldn't have. And Nalini wouldn't have to marry Zacchaeus...

Then he realised his life hadn't been all that wonderful before this had happened. He'd been racked with guilt about his wife, and he'd felt so terribly alone. And though the guilt was still there now—more pressing, perhaps—at least he no longer felt alone.

Because he had Leyna.

The realisation had him shaking his head. To keep himself from thinking of it, he went back down to his library. He checked that Leyna had left Mattan safely and, when that was confirmed, called for Nalini. He used the minutes before she arrived to prepare his words, but nothing he came up with made *Would you like to get married to our enemy to protect the alliance?* sound good.

Nerves settled heavily in his stomach, even when Nalini bounced into the room with her usual energy.

'You look like hell,' she said cheerfully, flopping down onto the couch.

Xavier gave her a sour look. 'It's called running a kingdom.'

'*And* you're in a bad mood. This is fantastic.' She grinned at him and he couldn't help his smile. 'How are things with Leyna?'

His lips straightened. 'Fine.'

'Really?' Nalini's eyebrows rose. 'Things are *fine* between you and the woman who broke your heart—excuse me, your fiancée?'

He was suddenly grateful he'd kept the possible pregnancy to himself. 'You're making it sound—'

'Complicated?' She grinned. 'It is complicated, though, isn't it?'

'You have no idea.' But she would. Soon. He just needed to find a way to tell her about it. But, before he could, she straightened and her expression lost its amusement.

'I was actually glad you called. I wanted to know how you were handling all of this. And truthfully. Not the rubbish answers you give us all at breakfast.'

'As well as can be expected, I guess,' he answered truthfully, and ran a hand through his hair. 'How *should* you handle a threat against your kingdom forcing you to come face-to-face with everything you've struggled with in your past?'

'You've been through worse,' she reminded him softly, and he nodded.

'Yes, I have.'

'But that doesn't mean things aren't bad now. Especially if you still feel something for Leyna.' When he didn't say anything, Nalini's eyes widened. 'You *do* still feel something for her. I knew it!'

'I loved my wife, Nalini.'

'Your wife's dead, Xavier,' she said gently, though the words still sent a ripple of unhappiness through him. 'You can't keep living your life as though she isn't.'

'I can't just move on either. Especially not with the woman everyone accused her of replacing.' He shook his head. 'Especially not with the woman *she* always accused me of wanting. I won't do that to her. I *can't* do that to her.'

'I know you don't want to hear this, but

love is stronger than duty.' Nalini's voice was firmer now. 'Leyna was love. Erika was duty.'

'I loved Erika, too.'

'I know you did. But it wasn't the same, was it?' She waited but he didn't answer. 'Being with Leyna now. How does that feel?' Again, he didn't say anything. What could he say? That she was right? 'I don't care if you won't tell me, Xavier, but you should at least be honest with yourself.'

He blew out a breath. 'Things *are* complicated,' he said, and she smiled.

'You can tell me I'm right when we're on the other side, talking about how glad we are that we're through it.'

It reminded him of what he'd called her there for. He cleared his throat. 'You must have heard that Zacchaeus paid us a visit today.'

Her smile sobered. 'Yes, I did. And I saw him. Briefly, in the castle. He looked like he'd just left a storm behind.'

'I'm afraid he wants to bring you into the storm with us.'

Xavier explained, as briefly and as clearly as he could, what the meeting had been about. He felt her entire demeanour become serious—an obvious change since she was always so full of happiness—and told her that the decision was completely hers.

'I'd like to talk to him.'

'About what?'

'I want to know how serious he is about this.'

Sensing her reluctance to talk to him about it, he nodded. 'Sure. If we decide to do this, you can talk to him.'

'When will that decision be made?'

His mind raced. 'Leyna and I have to first talk through the implications of both options.'

She nodded. 'Would you let me know as soon as you've made your decision?'

'Your feelings about this will affect that decision, Nalini.'

'I'll do it,' Nalini said softly. 'I want to talk to him about it first, but I'll do it.'

'Are you sure?'

'It's my duty, Xavier, and you're my King.'

'You know that's not—'

'Relevant here?' She smiled. 'I know. But, like it or not, this *is* my duty. Especially if it protects Mattan.'

He walked to her and pressed a kiss on her forehead. 'We're lucky to have you as our Princess.'

She gave a soft laugh. 'We're lucky to have you as our King.' There was a beat of silence, and then she said, 'And, as one of your people, Xavier, I want you to be happy.'

He sighed. 'Nalini—'

'Erika would have wanted you to be happy, too, Xav.' Nalini stood now. 'I know your relationship wasn't traditional, and that things were harder because of your fertility problems, but she loved you.' She patted his cheek. 'She would have wanted you to be happy. Even if it was with Leyna.'

Nalini left him wondering whether that was really true.

CHAPTER THIRTEEN

IT WAS A strange thing, waiting for the results of a pregnancy test. Leyna's doctor had taken the blood sample a few hours ago, and he'd told her to expect the results in the next hour. The nerves sat in her chest, reminding her that when the news came it would change her life.

Once upon a time, a long time ago, she'd wanted a child. She'd wanted a family and she'd wanted to rule. But then she'd realised that ruling had been more important than her desire for a family. Yes, she'd got there because she'd been afraid of losing Xavier—of disappointing her kingdom—and had pushed him and those dreams away. But when she'd thought about it, she'd realised she wouldn't have had the time to be a queen *and* a mother. Not the mother she wanted to be anyway.

Not a mother like hers had been.

Leyna poured herself a glass of water and raised it shakily to her lips. She'd had to face all her issues in the last few weeks. All of the emotions and memories she'd hidden in the crevices of her mind had burst out, demanding her attention. It had only been a matter of time before she thought about her mother, really.

And, considering the news she was waiting to receive, it wasn't a surprise that that particular issue had come up now. But it didn't mean that she wanted it to. Not when it had her wondering, a little out of the blue, whether abandoning a child could be a genetic trait. Whether putting her own needs above her child's was something she'd learnt without her knowing it.

Whether she could serve her kingdom and be the mother that her child deserved.

'Leyna.'

The glass almost fell out of her hand, but she corrected quickly and only a little water splashed out onto her fingers.

'I'm sorry, I thought you were expecting me.'

'I was,' Leyna replied and set the glass down on a piece of paper, wiping her hand on the side of her dress. 'Just a little lost in thought.'

'I could see that.' Xavier stopped in front of her. 'Everything okay?'

'Perfect,' she said brightly. 'Just waiting to hear whether we're about to become parents.'

Nerves flashed in his eyes, and it made her feel better about her own. 'When will we know?'

'Any time now.'

She'd just finished speaking when the phone rang. It took a beat for her to move, but then she walked back around her desk and answered.

Then slammed the phone down after her doctor told her the results.

'Was that your doctor?' She nodded numbly. 'What did he say?'

She walked through her balcony doors then, desperately needing air. And, when she heard him behind her, she spoke without turning around.

'I'm pregnant.'

Before she knew what was happening, he'd pulled her into his arms. She could feel his body shaking—or was that hers?—and allowed herself to take comfort from him for one short moment. She wrapped her arms around him, letting her face rest on his chest. She closed her eyes and again felt dangerously close to tears.

Except this time she knew she could blame it on her hormones. Which, apparently, were in full swing despite her being only two weeks pregnant.

The reminder had her moving out of his arms and heading back into the library.

'You don't seem happy about this,' Xavier noted quietly when he joined her.

'That I'm pregnant and trapped in what will be a marriage of convenience?' She closed her eyes and then shook her head. 'I didn't mean that.' She took a breath, and then another, and forced herself to think rationally. 'I only meant that it's still early. This might not work out.'

'You mean you might miscarry our child? Is that what you want?' he asked, his voice low, though she could still hear the pain.

'Of course not! I'm just… I'm just in shock.' She offered him what she was sure was an unconvincing smile. 'I'm allowed to process.'

'Yes, you are.' He paused. 'But even if you are processing… It doesn't mean what you just said wasn't what you felt.'

'*Of course* I don't want to have a miscarriage, Xavier—'

'I was talking about you being trapped. Is that how you feel? Is that why you made that offer a week ago?' He walked closer to her, but stopped a metre away. 'You made it seem as though you were giving *me* an out, but maybe you were giving yourself one. And now you don't have it. Now,' he continued, gaining steam, 'you have to continue the charade of this marriage. You can't push me away now, afraid that I would walk away first—'

'That's *not* what I was doing.'

'No?' he asked. 'So you're telling me that you weren't scared I would suggest backing out of our alliance?'

Trapped, she found herself floundering. 'You didn't want Nalini to—'

'No, I didn't,' he interrupted. 'But that didn't mean I was just going to abandon you, or the promise we made to each other. To our kingdoms.'

'It wasn't a promise,' she said now. 'It was a *plan*. Plans change.' She closed her eyes, and turned away, but whirled back at him. 'Do you think this was how I *planned* to have a child? To be married?'

'Do you think this is how *I* planned to have a child and marry?' He took a step towards her now. 'You told me our responsibilities come first. That what's happening now.'

'But it *shouldn't*. It shouldn't come first.' The words were ripped from her. Ashamed, she sat down, giving her shaky legs some reprieve. 'I didn't mean that.'

'No, you did.' He took the seat opposite her. 'And it's fine.'

'It's not fine,' she nearly sobbed. 'I know my duty comes first. I believe it does.' But she was trying to convince herself of it, not him. There was a long stretch of silence after she'd said it, giving the guilt time to do its work. She lifted a shaky hand to her face and felt the guilt mingle with shame.

'Why is duty so important to you, Leyna?' Xavier asked quietly. 'And I'm not talking about you serving your kingdom or being responsible for your people's lives. I'm talking about *you*.'

'I… I don't know what you mean.'

'That's part of the problem.'

'Why is duty so important to *you* then?'

He threaded his fingers together and didn't meet her eyes, but answered. 'I think because it was a way to prove myself. To prove that I could be as good as my father. Or maybe to try and show them—my mother and grandmother—that we shouldn't be compared.'

Compassion poured into her. 'You shouldn't have been. Your father was a good man, and a great king. And so are you, but in a completely different way.'

'Except there was only one way in their eyes, and that wasn't the way I was.' His gaze lifted to hers. 'You know what they used to say to me. How they treated me. None of that changed when we stopped being friends.'

'I know.'

'In fact, it probably got worse.' She could see the struggle on his face, and only realised why it was there when he continued. 'When I married Erika, her expectations of me were added to the ones I already had no hope of living up to.'

'What do you mean?'

'For most of our marriage Erika was miserable. She didn't want this life. Our life.' Emotion—hurt, regret—flashed across his face. 'I shouldn't have agreed to marry her.'

The years that they hadn't been friends faded away so that when she reached out to take his hand it was as his best friend, not as the woman who'd agreed to marry him. 'You feel like you should have protected her from what being royal meant.'

'Yes.' The admission was said in a hoarse voice.

'Could you have?' she asked, knowing that he wouldn't have asked it of himself. 'Because you told me that neither of you had a choice. Not really. So could you have said no to your King and your family and refused to marry her?'

'That's not what I meant—'

'No, but that's what protecting her would have entailed, Xavier.' She let that sink in and then continued softly, 'And if she really wanted to, she could have protected herself, too. She was an adult, and she was a part of your circle. She must have known what she was getting herself into when she said yes.'

'No one from the outside can know what they're getting themselves into, Leyna.'

'Maybe not entirely, but she saw what was required of you. She must have known it would be required of her, too.'

'It wasn't that simple.'

'I know that. We've spoken before about how that term doesn't apply to us. But I think you're making it more complicated than it has to be.'

'You don't understand.' He pushed up from his seat, and she saw she'd made him angry.

'Did she make you happy?' she asked instead of pushing, because she needed to know, as much as she wanted to distract him.

'We got along well. Really well,' he said with a frown.

'And that was basically the same as being happy.' It wasn't a question. 'For the kind of relationship you had, with all the factors influencing it, it was enough.'

He would need to think about that, she knew. And so would she. She hadn't allowed herself to feel hope when Nalini had first told her about Xavier's unhappy marriage. And she'd reminded herself of that after Xavier had told her his marriage had essentially been arranged.

It had been easy to do when it was clear he was still so consumed by whatever had transpired in his relationship with his wife.

But now she let the idea soothe some of the hurt she still carried about him moving on from her. Not because Xavier and Erika hadn't been happy together—Leyna believed, as she'd told him, that happiness for people like them wasn't black and white. But because he hadn't got over *her* as easily as she'd thought he had.

She felt shame at that, but it still alleviated some of her own pain. But *that* realisation had the emotions that had been hidden behind her hurt become more pressing, and the relief was short-lived. Especially when she realised one of those emotions was the very hope she'd suppressed when he'd first told her about the circumstances of his marriage.

It worried her. And made a different kind of panic than the one she was used to throb along with her heartbeat.

'What you had with Erika,' she forced herself to say, making sure her voice was calm and matter-of-fact. 'That's more than most people get, Xavier.'

'Maybe for us, Leyna. But not for people like Erika. She was *normal* before she married me. And normal people should have a chance at real happiness.'

'She *was* happy, Xavier. That light I saw between the two of you on your wedding day? That was happiness. That was someone who was happy with the choice she'd made. Why don't you want to believe that?'

'Because she didn't die happy, Leyna,' he choked out. 'And that was my fault.'

CHAPTER FOURTEEN

'I FAILED HER.' Now that he knew he wasn't infertile, he felt the truth of those words even more. 'I should have given her a child, Leyna.'

'Or she should have given *you* a child.' Leyna's expression was impassive. 'It was more important to you. You needed an heir. Mattan needed an heir. In fact, it was her civil responsibility.'

'That isn't fair.'

'No, it isn't, is it?' she told him mildly. 'I agree. And yet that's exactly what you're telling yourself.'

He was too stunned to feel betrayed by the trap. But it felt…strange to accept what she was saying. For so long he'd blamed himself for their struggle to conceive. It hadn't mattered that there hadn't been a medical reason indicating that either of them had been responsible. It had been almost…simple, *easy*, to accept the blame. Just as he had taken the blame for her unhappiness, for her struggle with being Queen.

It was the first time he'd considered either, and he didn't know what that meant. All he knew was that Leyna telling him she was pregnant had changed something. First, it had added to the guilt. But now, along with her telling him he was being unfair to himself...it had changed things. And because he didn't want to face what that meant right at that moment, he suddenly remembered how they'd reached this conversation in the first place.

'If I admit to being unfair to myself, would you admit that you're doing the same?'

She frowned, and he knew it was because of the question as much as the change in the direction of their conversation. 'What are you talking about?'

'This obsession you have with duty.'

She gave him a look. 'Really? We're engaged and about to become parents for the sake of our kingdoms and I'm the only one who has an obsession with duty?'

'At least I know *why* I'm obsessed. Why are you obsessed?'

'I'm not obsessed,' she said dismissively. 'I don't have a choice. It's different.'

'But you did have a choice.' He kept his eyes

on her face. 'You had a choice long ago, and you chose duty.'

'I told you why I did that.'

'Yes, and you were afraid then. But there's something more, Leyna, because you're afraid now, too.'

'Xavier, we don't have time for this.' She stood, and he saw the annoyance in her face and the set of her shoulders. But he also saw that it wasn't *only* annoyance. No, her face held the same expression that she'd had when she'd told him she was pregnant. And since he knew that news had terrified her, he wanted to know what was scaring her now.

'We have time,' he said in a serious voice. 'Tell me why duty is so much more important than love for you. Even though you admitted that it shouldn't be.'

'Duty is the most important.'

'Love is stronger than duty,' he replied, repeating Nalini's words.

'Is it, Xavier? Is it really? Because you chose duty over love when you married Erika. How was love stronger there?'

'Since I've already told you that, we both know you're deflecting.'

'So you're allowed to bring up things we've already spoken about, but I can't?'

'Still deflecting.'

'I'm *not* deflecting,' she snapped. 'I just don't want to talk about this right now. I've just found out I'm pregnant, for heaven's sake. I've listened to you speaking about the woman you replaced me with—'

'She was *not* a replacement,' he hissed, and saw her wince.

'No, of course she wasn't.' She closed her eyes. 'I'm sorry, Xavier, I shouldn't have said that.'

'But you did,' he replied in a hard voice. 'Because keeping this secret is so much more important to you than speaking about it.' He shook his head, the desire to get her to admit what was really going on disappearing. 'I'm trying, Leyna. I *have* tried since this entire situation began. But no more. I'm not putting myself through this any more.'

'Through what? Through trying to figure out the past? I *told* you there was no point in it. You can't be angry with me for that.'

'I'm not,' he answered, his anger seeping away, leaving only a bone-deep tiredness. 'But you're fooling yourself if you think that all of this is because of the past. Not ours, at least.'

When he saw she didn't understand what he meant, he told himself he would try one more time and then move on. This was for his child, he thought, and ignored the voice in his head telling him it was for him, too.

'You're carrying something around with you, Leyna. I don't know what it is, but it's there and you're using your responsibilities as Queen to coat it so you don't have to deal with it.' He gave her a moment to process his words before he continued. 'Of course, duty is important. But you were right when you said it earlier. It *shouldn't* be the most important thing. Not if we want to lead our people properly.'

'You think putting our happiness before our duties will make us better leaders?' she scoffed.

'No, but doing it the other way around doesn't either.' He realised the truth of his words as he spoke them, and felt something free inside him. 'I've done it the other way, Leyna. I know how that ends. And for a little while *that* made me a bad king. So yes, maybe I *do* think being happy will make us better leaders.' Again, he thought of the conversation he'd had with Nalini. 'And you know? I think our people would want us to be happy, too.'

She didn't respond, and silence grew between them for several minutes before he realised he was no longer needed—or wanted—there. He walked to the door, ready to leave, but before he did he said, 'You've always put duty first,

Leyna. Do you think doing that has made you the kind of queen you always wanted to be? If so, then fine, we'll go on to be dutiful spouses and parents. But if not…'

He left with the possibility his words had suggested hanging in the air.

Damn him, she thought furiously. Damn him for bringing up something she'd told him in confidence when he'd been her best friend.

For pushing when she'd told him not to.

For seeing right through her.

Leyna's hand itched for something to throw, but instead she walked to the balcony and breathed in the sea air. She'd seen her father do the same thing so many times. She didn't think he'd ever noticed, but she'd watched him all the time. Even as a young girl she'd known that she would one day take on his role, and it had made her perceptive.

And what she'd perceived had scared her.

The crown had taken her father away from her. He'd changed so drastically after his coronation that Leyna had known it had been because of the crown and what it meant. She'd told Xavier once that she hadn't wanted to turn out that way. She'd repeated it the day he'd proposed. And now Xavier was telling her she'd become exactly what she'd feared.

Oh, he hadn't said it so explicitly. He wouldn't. But she knew that was what he'd meant. And now she was worried that she had inherited the ugly sides of both her father *and* mother.

She pressed a hand on her belly at the thought, squeezing her eyes closed against the tears she had no power to stop. She desperately hoped that wasn't true. What would she be leaving her child with then? It had suddenly become incredibly important that she give her child more. He or she didn't deserve what Leyna had received. Her child deserved what she'd had at the beginning—supportive, caring parents who'd put their child first. Not what she'd ended up with.

She stilled, realising for the first time that there was something more important to her than duty. It shook her. So much that she barely made it back to the couch before her legs gave way. She took a breath, steadied herself and ignored the inner voice that screamed at her to ignore the realisation. She'd done that so often in the past that it had become her default, but she needed to think this through.

Her first thought was that Xavier was right. Clearly there was something in her focus—she refused to call it an obsession—on her duty that wasn't purely about duty. She saw now that it was partly because she hadn't wanted to turn out like her father. And she'd thought that zeroing in on her duty was how she was going to prevent that.

Her father had been a good king, but he'd not been the best father once he became King. So, she'd reasoned, if she didn't have a family to let down, she could focus on being Queen. It made sense in a cruel, ironic sort of way. Because, though she'd succeeded in being Queen and doing it well, it had turned her into the miserable person that her father had been.

And yes, she wasn't disappointing her family. But she was disappointing *herself*, because that wasn't the kind of queen she'd wanted to be. Or the kind of person.

Then there was her mother. Even the thought made her nauseous, so she knew how much it affected her. She shut her eyes against it, and brushed impatiently at the tears that kept on coming. She couldn't stop them. Not when she'd just realised why she'd placed so much emphasis on her responsibilities. Leyna hadn't wanted to be like her mother either. Not as a mother, and not as a woman.

Responsibilities meant something. But because Leyna hadn't had responsibilities other than the crown, she'd channelled her passion for that belief into ruling. Now she had more.

She had a child to think of. She had someone who deserved her love and respect—she wouldn't abandon them when they needed her the most. Or when the demands of the crown became difficult.

Love is a wonderful thing, but when you lose it you lose sight of what's important.

Her grandmother had been right. When Leyna had lost Xavier, she *had* lost sight of what was important. But that hadn't been duty. One day Leyna would forgive herself for thinking that. Because how could she not? Her grandmother, the closest family member she'd had left, had drilled it into her. She'd focused on duty so absolutely herself that Leyna had had no choice but to follow.

But no, what was most important was *love*. She'd convinced herself it wasn't and that she hadn't needed it when she'd pushed Xavier away. When she'd let her fears overwhelm her and overshadow her feelings. And then she'd forgotten how to love herself, and her dreams for her future.

Those dreams had been a balance between family and her royal duties. Those dreams had been filled with a family with Xavier. With them balancing their royal duties *together*.

Losing him had been the worst thing that had happened to her. Losing his friendship *and* his love. It had made her into a version of herself she hadn't wanted to be. And now, with their child on the way, she wanted to be better. She wanted to show her child what was important.

And since she'd just realised love was important, and that love included Xavier, she had a lot to think about.

For herself, and for her child's sake.

CHAPTER FIFTEEN

Xavier waited two days before he contacted Leyna again. He knew they were on a deadline with Zacchaeus, but forty-eight hours wouldn't change anything. At least that was what he hoped, and he would have dealt with it if something had come up.

But he needed time to think, to process after his last conversation with Leyna. And he'd wanted to give Nalini one more chance to back out before she made a decision that would change her life for ever.

Had he known how much *his* life would change when he'd agreed to the marriage and pregnancy of convenience with Leyna? If he had, he'd muted the warnings. He'd done what he'd thought was required of him. And that was what Nalini was doing now, stubborn in her decision to go ahead with the arranged marriage with Zacchaeus if that was what he and Leyna wanted.

He'd warned her. He'd told her all the things he wished he'd known before he'd made *his* decision. But she'd just given him a look and lightly told him that their experiences wouldn't be the same.

'You're getting married to your first love for the sake of the kingdom,' she'd told him. 'I'm getting married to a man I barely know. Obviously, I have the harder job here, so while I appreciate that our situations are similar, they're hardly comparable.'

And that had been the end of the conversation.

But the moment he'd found out Leyna was pregnant, he'd known their options were limited with Zacchaeus. Aidara and Mattan would have to negotiate with Kirtida, and face whatever the consequences would be. They'd find out the details in the negotiation, but that conversation would only happen once they told Zacchaeus of their decision.

Which would entail speaking with Leyna.

The thought of it had his heart racing, but he forced himself to make the call and was now waiting for Leyna to arrive. So, naturally, everything he'd wanted to avoid thinking about when it came to the woman who was carrying his child was now traipsing through his mind as casually as teens in a mall.

There was the happiness—the pure, unadulterated happiness—he felt about being a father. And, of course, the guilt that came along with it. He'd thought once that he would never become a father. He'd felt Erika's devastation—and his own—thinking they would never have a child. And with Leyna pregnant, so easily, too, he knew there would be guilt.

But it wasn't as consuming as it had been before. Perhaps because he'd realised that there were some things outside of his control. And, yes, also because Leyna had shown him that blaming himself or Erika for something that neither of them could logically take responsibility for was unfair.

But it had him thinking that struggling with the fact that there *was* a child was just as difficult for him as the fact that *Leyna* was carrying the child. He wasn't sure if *that* guilt would ever entirely go away either. For that to be a possibility, he would have to accept that Erika had loved him as much as Nalini said she had. And there was something inside him that just didn't quite believe that to be true.

He didn't like what that said about them or their marriage. Especially since he'd agreed with Leyna when she'd said he and Erika had been as happy as they could have been, given who they were and how they'd come to be together. Things had been complicated between them, and that was how he'd always remember it.

But that was why he was wary of getting involved in another complicated relationship. In another complicated marriage. More so now because there was a child involved. And, for the sake of his child, he would ignore the feelings he could now admit he had for Leyna. The feelings that had perhaps never really gone away. And maybe never would. But their marriage, their relationship, would be cordial and respectful for the sake of their duties—royal and parental.

He felt pretty confident in his convictions until Leyna walked through the door to his library in a beautiful blue dress with her hair falling freely around her face. It was as if his heart was mocking him for thinking he could be anything but in love with her.

That thought stole his breath, had him sucking in air like a dying man, and had her rushing to his side.

'Are you okay?' she asked, wrapping an arm around his shoulders.

'Yes,' he rasped and walked away, out of her embrace and away from that intoxicating floral scent she wore. And then he turned back to her.

'What upset you?' she asked, but he wasn't

completely listening to her. No, he was listening to the voice in his head telling him to kiss her.

He wanted to see whether he was fooling himself by believing they could be in an amicable marriage. He wanted to know if the feelings he'd only just allowed himself to acknowledge were in fact love.

But when he strode towards her, snaked an arm around her waist and touched his lips to hers, he thought only that he really, really wanted to kiss her.

Though he knew it was, it didn't seem like a terrible idea when he could feel her melting against him. When her mouth opened to offer more and her tongue plunged, taking more.

He wanted to pull back and enjoy her. To enjoy the way she looked in the soft sunlight streaming through the open balcony windows directly onto them. To savour the look of her, needy and womanly, in that beautiful blue dress with her hair framing her face.

In his arms.

But he didn't, too afraid that if he pulled back he would come to his senses—that *she* would come to hers—and stop before he'd had his fill.

Take, a voice whispered in his head, and he listened. He let his hands roam over her body. Up the sides of her, revelling in the slight curves, the tempting softness, and stopping just beneath her breasts.

He could feel her heart beating and smiled against her mouth when he thought her heart rate matched his. One hand slid up to cup the base of her neck and then pulled gently at her hair, angling her head so that *he* could now take, now give, more.

His mind, already hazy from their contact, went completely blank when her hands pulled his shirt from his pants. His body, already heated and wanting, ached more as she undid the buttons of his shirt, exposing his skin and torturing him as she started her exploration.

His heart sprinted towards an unknown finish line as her hands ran over his skin, heating his body until he thought he would combust. Her lips moved from his to kiss his jaw, his neck, her tongue joining to tease him. To drive him crazy. She lifted her head, smiling up at him in a heady way that had the same effect as her kisses.

And then she froze, and he saw the transformation in her eyes.

Lust and desire turned to fear and embarrassment. The colour in her cheeks faded so quickly he worried she would faint. But she just took a step back, and then waved a hand at him and turned away. It took him a moment to realise she wanted him to button his shirt and he made quick work of it, his body's denied desires making him edgy.

Making him ignore what his experiment had confirmed.

'I'm done,' he said tersely, and went to the decanter next to his desk for a drink—just as much for thirst as for sanity—and then he set the glass down and squared his shoulders.

'I'm sorry. I should have…' Her voice faded, and she looked more vulnerable than he liked.

'It wasn't you,' he replied. 'It was me. I wanted to—'

'You wanted to what?'

'Nothing.' What was the point in telling her? It wouldn't take away the dread or fear at the realisation of the extent of his feelings for her. In fact, it only added to it. Because if he told her, she would feel the need to respond. And he didn't want her to respond. 'We need to make a decision about Zacchaeus.'

Accepting the shift in his focus, she gave him a quick nod. 'What did Nalini say?'

'She'll do it.'

'You told her she didn't have to, though, right?'

'Of course I did,' he snapped. 'I even warned

her about all the delightful things she can come to expect.'

Her eyebrows lifted. 'Like moody men?'

'And women in denial,' he shot back, and then shook his head. Told himself to stay on topic. 'She's aware of what she's agreeing to. As much as she can be.'

'So we're negotiating,' she said. 'That's the best option we have, I suppose.'

'The safest one, too.'

She nodded, and then sank into the chair behind her. 'Does this mean the nightmare is over?'

He felt himself softening. 'I'm afraid not.'

'No, of course not.' She pursed her lips. 'Now we find out what trouble Zacchaeus has got himself—and us—into.'

'You know, when he told us that things were complicated on Kirtida, I believed him.'

'I did, too. He sounded sincere.'

'Like the Zacchaeus we knew.'

'Maybe,' she considered. 'But then, forcing your sister to marry him isn't entirely like the man we knew.'

'I don't blame him, though,' Xavier admitted. 'I hate that it's Nalini, but wouldn't you want to have the same guarantee as the other members of a three-way alliance?'

She was silent for a moment and then said,

'I think if this wasn't personal and we saw it completely from a business point of view, then yes, I'd agree. And I'd probably do worse if my kingdom was on the line.'

'And you did, didn't you?' It was a joke, but he'd felt his chest tighten at her words—at the reminder of her *duty*—and he didn't want to go there again. Perhaps to prove to himself that he could.

But then she settled a hand on her belly, a soft smile on her lips, and he felt as though someone had squeezed his heart in their hand.

It was such a simple gesture but it had all the pictures he'd fought off over the last two days reeling through his mind. Pictures of her with a rounded belly. Beautiful. Graceful. Strong. He imagined their first doctor's appointment, and hearing their baby's heartbeat for the first time. Touching her stomach to feel their child kick. Holding him or her for the first time.

He'd imagined it all so often when he'd been young, so in love with her that it had made him dream of a future that he suddenly felt incredibly lucky to have. Because of that, those pictures now felt like memories, not images of the future. And it told him that being in love with Leyna had never been a choice for him.

Knowing the effect of that on his marriage too was hard to accept. He'd tried to deny it, had thought he'd put the nail in its coffin when Erika had asked him about Leyna. How could he not? He'd been married and his wife had questioned his feelings for another woman. So he'd shunned them, painting what he'd felt for Leyna with shame and anger.

The light, the goodness his feelings now shone with, told him he'd turned a corner. But he wasn't entirely sure what to do about it.

'Is that all?' Leyna asked now, her eyes careful.

'No.' He took a breath. 'I want to talk about the kiss.'

She blinked. 'What?'

Since he'd been taken aback by it, too, he understood the reaction. But, now that he'd said it, he realised that his heart had prompted the words, showing him what he needed to do about those feelings. So he said it again.

'I want to talk about that kiss.'

'I… I don't think that's a good idea.'

'But I do.' He took a seat across from her. 'For a long time I thought I hated you.' He saw her wince, but told himself it would be worth it. 'I didn't, not really, but when you broke my heart I thought I did. I certainly blamed you for it, and the resentment that went along with that blame...' He released a shaky breath. 'It was intense—intensely negative.'

'Why...why are you telling me this?'

'I'm getting there,' he replied, and then continued before he lost his nerve. 'It was a...a shock, when you told me that you blamed me, too. And rightly so, I now realise. I should have seen how much you were suffering. How scared you were—'

'Xavier—'

'No, I'm not done. I should have been there for you, Leyna. I should have fought for you. I should have.'

'But I told you I didn't love you and gave you no reason not to believe me.'

'Except a twenty-year friendship that should have told me to at least try.'

'I shouldn't have blamed you,' she said softly. 'I was angry and—'

'Why are you giving me so much slack?'

'Why are you being so hard on yourself?' she shot back. 'Is it because you've finally realised how unfair you've been to yourself with Erika and now you're doing it with me?'

As soon as she'd said it, she regretted it.

'Oh, Xavier, I'm sorry. I shouldn't have—' She covered her face with a shaky hand and commanded herself to pull it together. But she felt so incredibly raw, so incredibly vulnerable after realising she loved him that she didn't want to delve any further into her emotions.

It might have been a cowardly thing to do, but she'd been brave enough already in facing her feelings that week. Perhaps even that year. She didn't need to think about the emotions swirling inside her after her realisation.

His face had lost some of its colour, but Xavier merely said, 'It was a fair assumption to make.'

She nearly laughed. 'No, it really wasn't.'

'Who's the one being too hard on themselves now?'

Leyna knew he was right, but she preferred being hard on herself than thinking about how long she'd ignored the fact that she wasn't over him. How long she'd pretended she didn't regret pushing him away. As though by creating a life for himself without her he'd only hurt her and not *broken* her.

She'd got over the rest—at least she would— but still having feelings for him, still being *in love* with him… *That* was a hard thing to accept.

It was also hard to ignore.

As was the fear pulsing inside her. She had no clue why it was still there after she'd realised—and admitted—that she'd pushed him away out of fear of losing him. But they were going to be married, for heaven's sake. She was *pregnant*. She wasn't going to lose him—at least not his presence, or his friendship, she thought, considering his current mood. So that sickening, alarming feeling in her chest made absolutely no sense.

'I think I should go,' she said, and shifted forward.

'I'm not done, Leyna.'

'You feel guilty for not accepting your part in the way things ended between us. You want to apologise. You're forgiven.' She stood.

'Let me apologise,' he said through his teeth in a voice she'd never heard before, and she lowered back down to the couch.

'Fine. Apologise.'

'I was getting there,' he growled, and then took a breath. The entire scene would have amused her if not for that feeling in her chest. 'I said I should have fought for you. But you know why I didn't, and then I couldn't.' She nodded. 'I'm sorry for that. For not, at the very least, telling you about it in person.'

Stunned, she nodded again.

'But as much as I wanted to forget you and the awful things I felt about you, I couldn't. Because those awful things… Well, they went away pretty quickly, Leyna.' His eyes shone with sincerity. 'And all I was left with was a terrible hurt that told me I still cared.'

'I'm sorry,' she apologised again, as she had that night on the beach. This time she said it in a whisper. But he shook his head.

'I'm not telling you this because I want you to feel bad, Leyna.'

'Then why are you telling me?'

'Because that day, almost a month ago now, that Zacchaeus didn't attend the banquet—' She held her breath at the emotion in his tone. 'I wasn't as unhappy with our plan as I should have been—' he paused for a beat '—had there not been a part of me that really wanted to marry you.'

CHAPTER SIXTEEN

LEYNA FELT AS though the world had slowed. Why else would she hear her heart beating in her ears? Or feel the pulse of it carry the blood through her veins?

She needed water, she realised, and moved to stand. But when she was on her feet, the ground opened beneath her and she found herself falling. Strong arms caught her before she landed, helped her to sit, and then a hand pressed her head between her knees.

'Breathe.'

Xavier's voice spoke from a distance but she obeyed, opening her mouth to suck in the air she'd only just realised she had stopped inhaling. After repeating it for a few minutes, she straightened and felt the blood rushing through her body again.

But then she looked at the concern on Xavier's face and felt it nestle again in her cheeks.

'I'm calling the doctor,' he said, and stood.

'No, Xavier, I'm fine.' She nearly stood, too, to stop him, but then realised that if she did and her head wasn't as steady as she felt, it would definitely have him calling for a doctor. 'Really, I'm fine.'

'What happened then? Was it the pregnancy?'

'No.' It was ridiculous to admit, but she went on, knowing it would be the only way to keep him calm. 'I stopped breathing.'

The look of disbelief on his face had a laugh tickling up her throat. 'I know, I know, it's not funny. But your face…' She bit her lip, thinking about what had caused her to stop breathing to sober herself.

'Was my admission such a surprise to you?'

'Yes. Yes, it was.' All amusement gone now, she frowned. 'There's no way you wanted to marry me, Xavier. You had years to redevelop a *friendship* with me and you didn't. You didn't want to marry me,' she repeated.

'I didn't admit it to myself, Leyna, but there was some subconscious part of me that did.'

'But the conscious part of you wanted to protect your kingdom. That's enough for me.'

It had to be.

'It's not enough for me.' He sat again, next to her this time. 'I thought this plan was a disaster at the beginning. A necessity, but a disaster nevertheless.' He paused. 'I told myself I'd get through it by making sure we had boundaries. By making sure that everything was strictly professional. Which is why I agreed to the artificial insemination.'

'But you kept pushing me,' she said, confused. '*You* were the one who kept going back to the past when we could have just kept things professional.'

'Because that plan didn't work. I kept wanting to fix the past so…so we could fix the future.'

'Because we were going to be married and become parents.'

'No, because my plans when it comes to you… Well, they never work.'

'I don't… I don't know what you mean, Xavier,' she said shakily. 'I think I should go—'

'I mean that I couldn't ignore my feelings for you, Leyna. I fought them all the way and, up to half an hour ago, I still did.'

'What changed?' she whispered.

'Seeing you touch your stomach.' He put his own hand on her abdomen, spreading heat through her body. When he moved it away, she felt a coldness that no one other than him could warm. 'You're carrying our child, Leyna. *Ours*. The miracle of it actually happening the way it did… I know how long it takes…and the fact that it didn't take that long for us? It feels like a sign.'

'Since when do you believe in signs?' she scoffed, and stood, her heart thudding, the fear beating along with it.

'Since my wife and I tried for over five years to get pregnant and it took *us* less than a month.'

She immediately regretted mocking him, and closed her eyes briefly before opening them again. 'This conversation seems to be filled with apologies, doesn't it?' she said softly. 'I'm sorry, Xav. Of course you can think it's a miracle or a sign. You can think about it in any way you like.' She paused, and felt her heart nudge her to ask, 'Are you okay with this, though? Me falling pregnant, and Erika…'

'I don't know,' he answered hoarsely. 'Honestly, I feel guilty about this whole thing. And I know that not having a child wasn't the fault of either of us. I can see that now, and it's made it easier, but that guilt…it hasn't entirely gone away.'

'That's okay,' she told him, taking a seat again. But she sat opposite him, afraid that being close to him would have her falling into the trap his honesty was weaving around them. 'It might never go away, Xavier, but that's fine, too. It's shows that you cared about her.' She reached over and squeezed his hand, but lifted it just as quickly.

'What if she didn't know?'

'That you cared about her?' Because she heard the hurt, she forced herself not to scoff. '*Of course* she knew. And she cared about you, too. She loved you.'

'You can't know that.'

'I can,' she said, and felt her heart twist in her chest. 'People who don't care enough, Xavier…they leave.' She knew that better than most. 'Why do you think she didn't? Because she could have. She could have walked away to a different—easier—life. But she didn't. She stayed. She stayed for you, because she loved you.'

And because his silence told her he still didn't believe her, she told him what she herself saw. 'You said you both got along. And, like I said, that would have been enough to live a content life. A happy life, even, for us. But honestly, I think she loved you.'

It didn't hurt to say it, perhaps because Leyna saw it from Erika's point of view for the first time. And she understood. Leyna had fallen so hard for Xavier. How could she have expected someone else not to?

'Maybe *she* felt like she was failing *you*, Xavier. Maybe she wanted to give you a child so badly that she blamed herself, just like you blamed yourself. And however things ended between you two…well, it could have been because of the strain of that.' When he looked up at her, she smiled. 'Whenever you doubt that she loved you, remember that she stayed. And that she wouldn't have wanted a child with you if she didn't love you.'

He'd never thought about it that way, he realised, and his mind raced to consider whether it could be true. He couldn't deny that trying to have a child had put a strain on their marriage, but maybe it hadn't been because *he'd* failed *her*. Maybe it *had* been because she thought she'd failed him.

Regret filled him immediately. It must have been an incredible pressure to marry into a royal family and struggle to provide an heir. He realised then that it would have been worse in *his* family, and that Erika wouldn't have been immune to his family's unreasonable expectations.

It seemed glaringly obvious now that she must have felt those expectations directed at her, too. She'd spent a lot of time with his mother and his grandmother. Plus, Erika would have seen their ease at being royal even though they'd both married into it, and her own struggles must have been magnified.

Was it any wonder that things had become worse between them before she'd passed away? That pressure must have grown each day, with each negative pregnancy test. Her lashing out, allowing him to take the blame for the infertility... All of it could have been coping mechanisms to deal with a life that she just couldn't fit into.

Including when she'd asked him about Leyna. She could have been comparing *herself* to a woman who'd always been put on a pedestal...

He would never know for sure, but this explanation felt...right. He wished he could have spoken to her one last time to comfort her. To let her know that he didn't blame her. To apologise for his part in it all. He closed his eyes, hoping that if she could see him—hear him— she would know how sorry he was.

It didn't magically absolve him of his part in the way things had ended for them. It didn't mean that he didn't still feel guilty about the feelings he'd harboured for Leyna. But it *did* help him to think that he'd made an effort to set those feelings aside for his marriage. For Erika. He'd tried to ignore twenty years of friendship and love so his marriage could have a chance.

It made him feel better, and suddenly Nalini's words came to his mind. *She would have wanted you to be happy.* If he let himself believe that, he knew what would make him happy. Leyna. But there was so much history there, so much hurt, so much denial that he wasn't sure…

She wouldn't have wanted a child with you if she didn't love you.

Everything inside him froze, and then heated with the feel-good warmth he'd only felt once in his life before.

One day, ten years ago, when Leyna had said yes to his proposal.

'Thank you for helping me see that,' he told her gratefully, and prepared himself to make her admit that she loved him, too.

CHAPTER SEVENTEEN

'YOU'RE WELCOME,' LEYNA ANSWERED.

His expression told her he'd just realised something he never had before. That realisation had comforted him, she saw, and she told herself that was all she'd wanted. For *him*. And ignored the voice in her head telling her he needed closure to move on.

Why would that be important to her? She knew where she stood with Xavier. At least she had before he'd told her that maybe there'd been a part of him that had wanted to marry her all along and that their baby was a miracle. But if she ignored that—just as she was currently doing—she knew where they stood. Theirs would be a political marriage and they'd give their child as much love as he or she could stand.

She was fine with that. Happy, even. As she'd realised over the last few days, the standard of happiness for them was lower than for others. Than for normal people, as Xavier had said. So she would balance all of her duties going forward, and be careful not to let any one of them become an obsession.

She nearly smiled when she realised that she'd finally admitted exactly what Xavier had asked her to. She considered telling him, but knew that if she did she would be opening a can of worms. She didn't want to go back to that conversation. She didn't want to think about feelings she couldn't identify—about *that* feeling still lightly pumping with her heart—and she definitely didn't want to think about how much she loved him.

One way to do that would be to get out of his company.

'So, which one of us is going to tell Zacchaeus the news?'

'Does it matter?' he asked with a smile. 'You and I are essentially the same person from now on.'

That feeling began to pulse harder in her chest again with his words, but she forced herself to respond in the same light tone as him. 'Oh, I don't know about that. I think we're still very much our own people.'

'Oh, I know that. We both do. But you know how people are. They'll begin to group us together until there is no Leyna and Xavier, only Leyna-and-Xavier.'

'But we won't let that happen, will we?' she replied shortly, and stood. 'I think I'll head back to Aidara—'

'Why does it bother you so much?'

Xavier's voice had become serious, and he was studying her. Had he been doing that all along? she wondered. Surely not. If he had been, it would mean he suspected it bothered her. That he'd been taunting her. That somehow he knew about how tight her chest had suddenly become.

'It doesn't bother me, Xavier.'

'Then why are you running away?'

'Haven't you learnt your lesson about pushing yet?' she asked lightly, but meant it.

'Yes, I have. I've learnt that pushing gets you to tell me the truth. And, considering the honesty I've given you this evening, the least you could do is offer me the same.'

'The least…' she repeated. 'I don't know what's got into you, Xavier, but I'm not sure I like it.'

'I wasn't sure I did, either. Not until a few minutes ago when you helped me realise how important it was to talk to someone.' He stood with her, and took her hands in his. 'The only perspective you have is your own, and sometimes… Well, sometimes it's tainted by your own experiences, your own issues, ones you don't even know you have.'

'I don't know what you're talking about,' she said and pulled her hands from his. She needed to get out, she thought, and headed for the door. 'I'll talk to you in a few days—'

'I love you, Leyna.'

She froze. Her heart pumped uncontrollably in her chest and she lifted a hand, rested it there in hopes of getting it to slow. She didn't turn back when she heard him walk towards her, and took a deep breath when she felt him behind her.

'Leyna, I said—'

'I heard what you said.' She whirled around. 'I heard what you said, you selfish, *selfish* man.'

His face twisted in surprise. '*What?*'

'I said you're selfish. And you are.' She stepped around him and began to pace the room. 'Just because you've had some sort of… revelation doesn't mean you get to do this to me.'

'Leyna, I don't know what you're talking about.'

'I'm talking about putting me in this position. Telling me you love me and expecting me to believe you.'

'But—'

'Because I can't believe you, Xavier. I can't. I did once, and look where that got me.'

'That's not fair,' he said, and she could hear the anger.

'Neither is this.' She stopped. 'And so I'm not going to accept it. None of it. Not the fact that you think this marriage was meant to be, and not the fact that you're in love with me. Because you're not.'

'I am,' he shot back. 'Don't you dare say that I'm not.'

'Even when it's the truth? Because, like I told you about Erika, Xavier, people who love you don't leave.'

'So you're blaming me for leaving? Again?' He shook his head. 'I thought we were past this, Leyna. And if I can't blame you for pushing me away, you can't blame me for walking away.'

'Yes!' she sobbed. 'Yes, I can. Because I loved you with all my heart and it broke me, it *broke* me when you left. I can't do that to myself again. I won't.' She wiped impatiently at tears. 'I won't do that to our child either.'

He watched her in silence and she turned away from him, not wanting him to see any more of the tears that had come from nowhere.

The anger inside her settled in the quiet, and she felt embarrassment take its place.

But she didn't have to deal with it in front of him and she walked to the door, only stopping when Xavier threw his body in front of it.

'Get out of my way.'

'No.'

'Xavier, I just want to… Please don't do this to me.'

'But this isn't me, Leyna,' he said seriously. 'This is you, and the fact that you think all of this is because of me leaving when in actual fact it's because of your mother.'

'No, it's not,' she said immediately. Automatically.

'Yes, it is,' he insisted. 'You keep saying that people who love you don't leave. And you know what happened with me—with our situation—was different, so this has to be about your mother.'

She shook her head, but didn't speak.

'Finding out you're going to be a mother, too, must have brought all these feelings back again, Leyna. And that's fine. Absolutely fine. But you have to deal with them.'

'There's nothing to deal with,' she whispered, and felt the tears roll down her cheeks.

'Oh, baby,' he said, and pulled her into his arms.

The sobs came then—heart-wrenching sobs that she couldn't believe were coming from her. It was as if something had loosened inside her and as she cried, as she felt Xavier's arms tighten around her, she realised it was the same thing that had been stuck in her heart, in her throat, since her last conversation with him.

She'd thought she'd dealt with it. She'd thought that it was just because she didn't want to be the same kind of mother her own mother had been. Because she wanted to give her child more. And, though that was true, the tears that wouldn't stop, the sobs that broke as much as they healed, told her there was more.

Since she was standing in Xavier's arms, refusing his love because of it, she knew it had something to do with him, too. But she only realised it when her sobs subsided, when the tears dried, what felt like hours later.

'I'm sorry,' she said, stepping back.

'You don't have to apologise,' he replied, and she saw his body tense, as though he wanted to move forward but couldn't.

She'd put up boundaries, she realised. Not intentionally. But by stepping away from him she was telling him she didn't want his comfort. And while that wasn't entirely true, it was probably for the best. Because until she got through what she had to say, she didn't want him distracting her with his touch.

She was about to excuse herself to find something to mop up the remainder of her tears when he offered her a handkerchief. It was so sweet, so gentlemanly, so *old-fashioned*, that she had to bite her lip to keep from smiling. She turned away from him, tidied up her face and took a deep, steadying breath before she turned back.

'I *do* have to apologise, Xavier. Because you're right, I have been taking this all out on you when it wasn't really about you.' She tilted her head, considered. 'No, that's not true. It was—*is*—about you, too. But only because I'm… I'm afraid. You make me afraid.' She took another breath. 'Just like you did ten years ago.'

He nodded. 'You were afraid you would lose me.'

'Yes, I was. But…' She bit her lip, closed her eyes, and then spoke before she lost the courage. 'I was also terrified you would destroy me.' She opened her eyes then, and saw him try to mask his surprise.

'Why?' was all he asked.

'Look what happened to my mother, Xavier.' She rubbed a hand under her neck and then fisted it there, grabbing the top of the dress she wore. 'She loved my father very much, and it destroyed her when he died. It made her forget her responsibilities to what had become her kingdom, her home, too.'

'And she ran from her biggest responsibility,' he said, and his eyes told her that he understood. 'You.'

She nodded slowly. 'Yes. I didn't see before, and perhaps never would have if you hadn't pushed. Don't get cocky about it,' she said with a small smile when she saw his lips curve.

'Never,' he promised, and her smile widened for a moment before sobering.

'I think it was more than running from her responsibilities. I think it was, plain and simple, that love destroyed who she was. It happened to my grandmother, too. She used to be happy,' Leyna said, suddenly remembering a time long ago when her grandmother had smiled. 'She never used to be the unsupportive, unkind person she is now. But she lost my grandfather, and then my father...' She lifted her shoulders. 'And she blamed love. And because I was afraid of so much—of the crown weighing as much on me as it had on my father, of loving you, of losing you, of having it all change me, *destroy* me, of failing—I think it was just easier for me to blame love, too.'

Leyna shrugged again. 'My grandmother

was the closest thing I had to a family—to the family I once had, Xav—that I just accepted what she said. And I pushed you away and focused on my duty, because duty was constant, stable. And if it changed me, at least it wouldn't destroy me. At least that's what I thought.'

'You've changed your mind now?'

'Yes. Because it *did* destroy a part of me. The one that longed—dreamed—for a life where family and duty were equally important. A life where I could be married to you and have our children and rule together.'

'But then it brought you that life anyway,' he said, and it was hard to ignore the hope in his voice, on his face.

'It did.'

'And you're not afraid any more? Of any of it?'

She lifted her eyes to his. 'I know what my life looks like if I live it in fear. I know what it looks like without you. I don't want to live like that any more.'

He walked towards her, stopping only a few centimetres away. 'Is that a declaration of love?'

'Yes.'

Hesitantly, she slid her hands around his waist and felt the ripple of his muscles beneath them. Her heart thudded.

'Tell me again,' she whispered.

He lifted a hand and brushed the hair from her face. 'I love you.'

'And you mean it.'

'I don't think I've ever meant anything more in my life.' His eyes shone with sincerity. With hope. With *love*. 'I love you.'

'And you're not just saying that because of the baby?'

'I'm not just saying that because of the baby. Though that does make me love you more.' His arms went around her now. 'You're going to be an amazing mother, Leyna. Just like you're an amazing queen.' He smiled at her. 'Our child will grow up to see a strong, compassionate woman be a mother and queen, and do both with the courage and grace I see in you.'

His words soothed a decades-old hurt, and she felt light. She felt *happy*. Real, genuine happiness that made her feel normal. The first real bit of excitement about her future, about her child, crept up her spine, settling in her heart. And she realised that the menacing feeling had disappeared from her chest.

'*And* our child—our children—will grow up according to standards we help them set for themselves. Of course, we'll teach them about what their duties will mean for their lives, but we'll allow them to figure it out for themselves. We'll guide, not compare. They'll be their own version of great. Just like you are. And we won't ever have to tell them to live up to you. Though they might want to,' she teased, and gave him a smile she hoped told him she loved him just the way he was.

'I love you, Leyna.'

'How many times are you going to say that?' she whispered, and felt her smile softening.

'As many times as it takes for you to say it back to me.' He pulled her in closer, and put his mouth next to her ear. 'Say that you love me, Leyna. Let's finally be happy together.'

'You'll have to say it again.' When he pulled back, she grinned at him. 'You said you'll say it as many times as necessary. So...say it again.'

He narrowed his eyes. 'I love you.'

'Again.'

'I love you.'

'One more time.'

He grinned now, and rested his forehead on hers. 'I love you, Leyna, Queen of Aidara.'

She bit her lip, holding back tears. If he asked her about it, she would blame it on the hormones. 'I *want* to tell you how I feel, but if I don't you'll have to tell me you love me on my every whim for the rest of your life.'

'What if I tell you I'll do that anyway?'

'That'll work,' she said, and felt her lips curving as her heart finally, finally felt whole again. 'I love you, Xavier, King of—'

His lips were on hers before she could finish.

CHAPTER EIGHTEEN

'ARE YOU SURE you want to do this?' Leyna asked Nalini. 'I know we've asked you that a million times, and you must be so annoyed by it at this point, but we can make a plan if you don't.'

Xavier didn't bother voicing his opinion on the matter. He'd already told Nalini that she could back out whenever she wanted to. As Leyna had said, they would deal with the repercussions if she did. But his sister was still being stubborn, insisting on going through with the plan.

'You want me to disappoint my future husband when he's on his way here? Right now?' Nalini teased, but Xavier heard the nerves in her voice. 'Let me do my part for the kingdom. For the alliance. I serve our people, too, you know.'

'Of course I know,' Xavier answered her. But he couldn't keep himself from adding,

'You do still have a choice in this. Now that we've entered into discussions with Zacchaeus about the Protection clause, we know Kirtida is facing sanctions from Macoa. We could use that as leverage to get him—'

'No, Xavier,' Nalini said firmly. 'That's not the way we do things.'

His lips curved into a half-smile. 'You still think you know better than me, don't you?'

'I know the kind of king you are,' she corrected. 'That isn't it.'

When he looked over at Leyna, she lifted her shoulders. 'Nalini's right. Besides, if Kirtida faces sanctions from Macoa, it impacts Aidara and Mattan, too. The alliance dictates our trade deals.'

'What concerns me about it is that Macoa knows that,' Xavier said, not for the first time. But it made him feel better to say it out loud. 'So their threat to impose sanctions on Kirtida is essentially a threat against the alliance.'

'Which means that negotiating with Zacchaeus is the best option,' Leyna replied, not for the first time either. 'Not blackmail.' She winked at him, and he felt his heart contract in the way it always had with her.

He knew that Macoa threatening Kirtida with sanctions didn't make sense. They had been an ally and business partner to the Alliance of the Three Isles for decades, and Zacchaeus' explanation that their gripe with Kirtida was personal hadn't been enough for Xavier. Especially since Xavier suspected, after dealing with Zacchaeus over the last week, that it had something to do with the coup that had started it all.

But Nalini was right. He wasn't the kind of king who would betray those who trusted him. And, to all intents and purposes, it seemed that Zacchaeus did trust him. Not enough to give them the details of the personal issue Macoa had with Kirtida, but enough to reveal that there *was* a personal issue. And to negotiate with them on how best to protect their kingdoms in light of it.

It seemed that Xavier and Leyna could trust Zacchaeus, too. He *had* given them the time to discuss their decision—or, in reality, to wait for the pregnancy test results—including the two days Xavier and Leyna had taken to sort through their personal feelings. He'd also told them the threat from Macoa had only been made once, and that though there had been no actions since to indicate they would act on it, he believed they would.

Xavier had no choice but to trust him. And if he was honest with himself, he had no reason *not* to believe him. Zacchaeus had been upright in their dealings since he'd made contact, and Xavier believed the reason he hadn't done so earlier *was* complicated, as he'd told them.

But until he reaffirmed Kirtida's place in the Alliance of the Three Isles, as all new kings were required to do, Xavier would be wary. Especially as the man had insisted on marrying his sister first.

'We've already announced the engagement, Xavier,' Nalini reminded him.

'Engagements can be broken.'

'Yes, they can.' He saw something in her eyes that had him wondering what he didn't know, but it was gone so quickly he thought he'd imagined it. 'But our kingdoms—both of them—' she smiled at Leyna '—have responded positively to this. It's a sign of a renewed alliance and, along with your engagement, soothes concerns.'

'But he hasn't signed the documents yet,' Xavier told her.

'Which is why I'm going to live on Kirtida under the guise of planning this wedding.'

After they'd told her what they'd decided regarding Zacchaeus, Nalini had called the King of Kirtida just as she'd told Xavier she would. When she'd returned, she'd told Xavier of this plan. It had worried him even more, but he knew that that worry would probably never cease.

But, as she'd reminded him, she was a grown woman and she could make her own decisions. And she'd made this one.

'I'll find out whether his intention of signing the documents on our wedding day is true.'

'It will be after all the details of the Protection clause are hammered out, too,' Leyna added.

'But still before yours,' Nalini replied. 'Our marriage is slightly more urgent if we take politics into consideration.'

'Oh, definitely,' Leyna replied smoothly, though he could see the amusement in her eyes. They hadn't told anyone about their pregnancy, both agreeing that it would be better not to disrupt the peace that had settled in their kingdoms once their people had heard about Nalini's engagement. Besides, it felt good keeping that news to themselves as their little secret.

'It'll be exciting,' Nalini said now. 'My own little adventure.'

'I thought you'd learnt your lesson about adventures.'

Her eyes flashed and though he wasn't happy referring to the time she'd left the castle as a teenager on an 'adventure' and had had to be rescued by the castle's guards, he needed her to be careful.

'You're no fun, Xavier,' she replied lightly, not taking him on for bringing it up. Now he *knew* she was nervous. But he didn't have time to ask her about it when his private secretary knocked on the door and told them Zacchaeus was on his way up.

'Last chance,' Xavier told Nalini. Her eyes had gone serious again, and she offered him a small smile before shaking her head.

'It's for Mattan, Xavier. That's enough for me.'

She straightened her shoulders and faced the door. Pride surged in him, and he couldn't place whether it was as a brother or as a king. Nalini was strong, he thought. She *had* learnt her lesson, and it had made her even stronger. She would take care of herself. And though he would still worry, he clung to that.

Zacchaeus was wearing all black when he entered, and Xavier felt a flash of annoyance. Was he trying to intimidate them? Why would he need to? He should have made more of an effort to make Nalini feel comfortable, Xavier thought, frowning.

He felt a hand slip into his then, and looked down into Leyna's eyes. Immediately some of the tension seeped from him, and he squeezed her hand. Together, they faced Zacchaeus.

'I'm glad you've agreed to this,' Zacchaeus said, his eyes revealing none of his emotion. He'd been speaking to Leyna and Xavier, but Nalini answered him.

'Actually, *I* was the one who agreed to it. You're marrying me, remember?'

Xavier watched something spark in Zacchaeus' eyes, but he didn't know if it was appreciation or annoyance. Again, he reminded himself that his sister could handle herself. Hadn't she just proved she was more than capable in a few words? This had been her decision. And it would be her decision whether she wanted to see it through, too.

Nalini hugged Leyna and whispered something into her ear that made Leyna's eyes glisten. Then his sister pulled back and hugged him.

'Call me,' he told her in a low voice. 'Call me whenever you need me.'

'I will,' she responded, her voice thick with emotion. But when she pulled back, her face was clear.

'Let's go,' Nalini said to Zacchaeus, but he frowned.

'Don't you want to say goodbye to your mother and grandmother?'

'I already have,' she answered. 'So let's get to it.'

Zacchaeus seemed taken aback for a moment, but he nodded to Leyna and Xavier and then they were gone.

Silence covered the room for minutes after they left. Leyna moved from his side to face him, sliding her hands around his waist and resting her head on his chest. Despite the emotion of having his sister leave with a man he still didn't know if he could trust, Xavier couldn't help the warmth spreading through him.

He held the woman he loved in his arms. They would have a child—be a family—in just over eight months. Their kingdoms were safe, and his sister's actions would ensure that if the time came when that wouldn't be the case, the Alliance would face it together. And though his feelings about Erika were still complicated, he felt as though he'd got some closure. Though he would worry about Nalini, he had to trust that she could handle herself.

Taking all of it into consideration, Xavier couldn't deny that his life was better than it had been in years.

'She'll be okay,' Leyna said, breaking the silence.

'I know.'

'She has her bodyguards, too, so she'll be safe.'

'I know that, too.'

'She's putting her kingdom first, Xavier.' Leyna leaned back. 'It's the same decision we made weeks ago. Perhaps even nobler because she didn't have ulterior motives.'

'I know.' But she'd got him to smile. And then he sighed. 'I'll worry.'

'I know.' She mirrored the grave tone he'd uttered the words in.

His lips curved again. 'Are you mocking me?'

'Never,' she said solemnly, and then walked to take a seat on his couch and patted the seat next to her.

But he shook his head. 'What do you think you're doing?'

She frowned. 'Sitting down?'

'You can't sit down, Leyna.'

He walked to the couch and scooped her into his arms. He'd discovered he liked the feeling of carrying her. It was a tiny way of showing her that he could, and would—and not just physically. Even when she made sounds of annoyance, as she did now.

'What are you doing?'

'We have somewhere to be.'

'And you couldn't have let me walk there?'

'I could have,' he said, and carried her through the door. 'But it wouldn't have been nearly as fun.'

She gave him a look that had him smiling, but she asked, 'Where are we going?'

'I owe you something.'

'If you don't tell me, you're going to owe me a lot more—' She cut off when he walked outside into the castle's garden. Though he'd felt fairly confident when he'd made the arrangements, he held his breath, waiting to see her reaction.

He'd filled a gazebo with flowers. White roses and pink lilies—her favourite—spilled over the sides, creating an image he'd hoped would be romantic. He set her down on a path of white and pink petals, leading down to the front of the gazebo.

Too nervous to wait any longer, he pulled her in and began to sway with her though there was no music. He felt her heart thud against his chest—though it could have been his, he thought, considering what he was about to do.

'What…what is all this?'

'Don't you know?' he asked, and twirled her around before pulling her close again.

'It looks romantic.'

He laughed. 'It's supposed to be.'

'Are you trying to soften me up, Xavier?' she asked in a mock stern voice.

'Is it working?'

She rolled her eyes, and then laughed breathily. 'You know it is.'

'Good.'

They swayed a bit longer and he leaned back to see her eyes closed, a small smile on her face. It was time, he thought, and drew back, taking her hands in his.

'Do you remember what you said to me when I gave you this ring?' He lifted the hand that wore the engagement ring and brought it to her lips.

'That you shouldn't hand it to me like it was a mint?'

He chuckled. 'Yes, that. You also asked me whether I had it made for our fake engagement. I didn't,' he admitted. 'I had it made for the real one, ten years ago.'

He watched as she opened and closed her mouth a few times, and then she whispered, '*Before?*'

'Long before. It was actually after one of our days at the beach. I was complaining about my family, as usual, and you were comforting me about it. As usual,' they said together, and smiled at each other. His nerves disappeared. 'And I remember thinking that I'd have the ring made so that when you were ready—when you would finally let me tell you I loved you—I would be ready, too.'

She bit her lip and blinked a few times, quickly.

'Are you—'

'No, you will not ask me whether I'm crying,' she interrupted him. 'You don't get to make me pregnant and then question what happens when I am.'

'*Technically*, that's true, but—'

'Whose fault is that?' she asked wryly. 'I've told you—'

'And I've told you that I want to wait.' He interrupted her this time. 'I want to give you rose petals and champagne. Non-alcoholic, of course. On our wedding night.'

'It isn't such a big deal.'

'It is, to me. And you know it is for you, too.' He tilted her chin up so she could look up at him. 'You waited for me, Leyna. I'm going to make sure we do it the way we were supposed to. The way you wanted us to.'

She shook her head, but he saw a tear roll down her face. 'I regret telling you that.'

'I don't,' he said, and kissed her forehead. 'I love knowing that you're mine. *Only* mine.'

'And now I *really* regret telling you that.'

He laughed, and wiggled the ring off her finger. 'The real reason we're here is because I owe you a proposal, Leyna.' He got down on one knee and offered the ring to her as he was supposed to have done ten years ago. 'I wouldn't recommend political turmoil to anyone, but I have to say it worked out *really* well for us.'

He smiled when she giggled. It was a happy sound that he knew he wanted to hear for the rest of his life. 'I'm glad we got this second chance at a life together. That our dreams of having a family, having each other and ruling have finally come true. So, to make it all official… Will you marry me, my Queen?'

There were no tears when she said yes, and he slid the ring onto her hand and kissed her, before pulling back and narrowing his eyes.

'Why aren't you crying?'

'Because I'm stronger than my hormones,' she teased, and then sobered. 'Because I want to remember this moment—that picture of you on your knee—for the rest of our lives together, and it wouldn't have been clear if I'd cried.'

He stared at her, and then laughed as he pulled her in. 'You're incredible, you know that?'

'Yes.' She smiled.

'And you're going to marry *me*.'

'Well, you *did* ask nicely…'

He smiled at her, and then shook his head. 'I won't take my second chance with you for granted, Leyna. I'm going to spend my life giving you everything you deserve.'

She rested her hand on his cheek. 'You've already given me more than I could imagine. I love you.'

'I love you, too,' he answered, and sealed the promise—their dream come true—with a kiss.

* * * * *

*Look out for the next
royal romance story in the*
CONVENIENTLY WED,
ROYALLY BOUND *duet*

FALLING FOR HIS CONVENIENT QUEEN
Coming soon!

*If you enjoyed this story check out these
other great reads from Therese Beharrie*

*THE MILLIONAIRE'S REDEMPTION
A MARRIAGE WORTH SAVING
THE TYCOON'S RELUCTANT
CINDERELLA*
All available now!